How to Sparkle!

A Magnolia Bluff Novella

How to Sparkle!

A Magnolia Bluff Novella

Leslie Kirby Devooght

Lanier Price
PUBLISHING

ISBN 978-1-967524-02-0 (paperback)

ISBN 978-1-967524-03-7 (e-book)

Library of Congress Number: 2025921971

Lanier Price Publishing. Jacksonville Florida

For Kirby. While life in the middle brought its own share of struggles, I hope you understand the blessing you are to our family and the world. May you always remain full of passionate idealism and big-hearted compassion.

Chapter One

As my plane barreled toward earth, I squeezed my eyes shut and grasped the back of my arms under my legs in the brace position like the flight attendant had instructed only a couple of hours before.

Would it even help when I crashed?

Unlikely.

Even though my jet wasn't actually plummeting toward a stone cliff, the result would be the same when I was the reason the biggest project of my career crashed and burned and exploded and—

I gasped as the wheels of the plane bounced before speeding down the runway of the Savannah, Georgia, airport in what could only be described as a textbook landing. If I hadn't known better, I'd have thought the pilot was messing with me by performing the smoothest landing ever.

"Honey, you're going to be okay. Bless your heart. We're just fine." Virginia, the unsuspecting, but very kind woman who'd had the misfortune of scoring the seat next to me and who I'd decided would make an excellent career coach, rubbed my back.

But since she taught preschool to three-year-olds, she probably wasn't the best person to give me job advice. Although given my current state of immaturity, little Susie was probably more prepared to lead the renovation team than I was. I bet Susie, with all her three-year-old bluster, could organize an entire kitchen in the corner of the classroom and set a perfect table with a centerpiece that would both anchor the room and give it a sense of whimsy. I, on the other hand, would choose all the wrong pieces of the plastic place settings, and it would look like a chaotic mess.

For months, my design partner, Wren, and I'd worked with our clients planning the renovation of their house, but the actual construction had just started at Magnolia Bluff. Our clients' development would transform the abandoned property into a retreat for overworked executives. The Retreat at Magnolia Bluff project was a huge undertaking, and anything could—and probably would—go wrong.

Because I couldn't do this.

I couldn't lead this team. If I'd learned anything in the last twenty-six and a half years of my life, it was that I'm a follower. Sometimes a cheerleader. Sometimes a top-notch assistant. But never, ever a leader.

And while I might be okay in the physical sense, the likelihood of my being *okay* was declining as if I were on that metaphorical malfunctioning airliner. My overactive imagination continued to spew unbelievably vivid worst case scenarios like one of Virginia's students with a stomach virus.

"We're pulling up to the gate, Zoe." Virginia squeezed my shoulder. "Why don't you take a few more of those deep breaths we talked about and don't forget to count to three before you blow out all the bad thoughts." She swore these breathing exercises helped calm her feistiest students.

I released the death grip I had on my arms and inhaled as I straightened. *One, two, three.* I exhaled.

"Very good." She nodded. "Now, remember, you have everything you need to do this job. Your boss has faith in you. Your clients have faith in you. And Wren has faith in you. You just need to have faith in yourself."

Her words eased the tornado inside me to a more manageable storm, but could I do it? Unfortunately, I didn't have a choice. I couldn't expect

Wren to abandon her family days after her grandmother's funeral. Even if that's exactly what her grandmother wanted her to do. In fact, she'd made Wren promise to come to Magnolia Bluff, but Wren decided that didn't mean she needed to come at the same time as me.

I rolled my shoulders, trying to release the tension. "Thank you. I'm sorry I've been such a bother."

"Honey, you haven't been a bother at all, and I'm going to be praying for you."

"I'll definitely accept all the help I can get." Because I was going to need a miracle of biblical proportions if I was going to pull off this renovation. At least Wren would only be a phone call away. We'd designed everything together, and she always treated me like an equal, but she was the one in charge. I loved how we worked, brainstorming ideas and searching out the right pieces for our interior design projects. Our aesthetics weren't exactly the same, and I was happy to add a little sparkle to Wren's designs and grateful that she made the final decisions.

Virginia patted my knee. "Don't sell yourself short. From what you've told me, you have everything you need to be successful. Now, straighten your headband. It's gone cattywampus, and we don't want Brad worrying that you don't feel up to the job. Remember: if all else fails, smile. It increases your face value."

I giggled before I sucked in my cheeks. This was not good.

"What's wrong? It's okay to laugh. It might relieve some of your stress."

"Not for me. When I'm nervous, I giggle, and if I get started"—a high-pitched round of giggles burst from me—"I can't control them." I clenched my teeth together as my insides quivered, trying to release the energy that would certainly be audible if it escaped. I pressed my lips harder as the ticklish sensation neutralized.

When the bell chimed from the front of the plane, the people around us stood, but even with Virginia's encouragement, I didn't feel any rush to meet my fate. Even though my immediate future included Brad Chastain, the general contractor for the project, who'd be waiting in the terminal to drive me to Magnolia Bluff. We'd only met over video calls, and he was nothing short of swoon worthy. From his natural good looks to his melodious drawl, he dripped Southern charm. Wren and I'd dubbed him H.B., short for Hot Brad. I squished my lips together to stop more laughter threatening to send me into hysterics.

As our fellow passengers shuffled down the aisle, Virginia released her seatbelt. "From what you've said, Brad shouldn't make you nervous."

While she might be right, because he'd seemed more into Wren, meeting him in person had my stomach doing flips. Maybe if I simply enjoyed the eye candy or focused on Brad's other attributes, I could control my nerves.

"I'm not sure if I have the ability to compartmentalize my emotions right now, but I also don't think I have a choice." I slid my headband into place like it was a gladiator's helmet.

"Good girl." Virginia rose and retrieved her roller bag from the overhead compartment. "I'm sure once y'all get working, everything will run smoothly, and you'll laugh about how worried you were."

"We'll see." I grabbed my vintage fuchsia purse from under the seat. I'd chosen it because it reminded me of the azaleas that Brad promised would be blooming during our stay in the Low Country. That's how he described this area of Georgia. I'd never heard the term before, but after a quick online search, I learned that it's the geographical and cultural area of South Carolina and Georgia's coastal plains. Exploring the region was one of the things that Wren and I'd been excited about, but now she'd only be here for a couple of days, and we'd have to work the whole time. I followed Virginia down the aisle and into the airport.

"I'd offer to meet Brad with you, but my husband is meeting me outside, and we have to hurry to an event at church."

"Please don't tell me I've made you late. I'm sorry."

She glanced at her watch. "No worries. We'll be right on time. I like to check for anyone who may be new or not have a group. It probably won't come as a surprise to you, but I like making people feel welcome and included."

"And you're very good at it. I don't know how I'd have gotten through that flight without you."

"You're just feeling overwhelmed, and I enjoyed hearing about your job and the renovation. You aren't in as bad a position as you think. You just need to keep the right perspective and remember those breathing exercises."

"I will."

Virginia pulled her buzzing phone from her purse. "It's my hubby. I need to take this. Good luck with everything, Zoe." She picked up speed, heading to the exit.

And then there was Brad. And oh, my gold glitter, he was something to behold. My feet stalled as my mouth fell open, and I blinked. In-person-Brad could only be described as something between a Greek god and Paul Bunyan. Burly in all the best ways, tall and broad with muscles that pressed against his clothes, unwilling to be hidden. His hair was not blond and not brown, but golden. I slapped a trembling hand over my chest as his piercing blue eyes met mine.

Then he did it—he smiled, and my insides melted, and my knees actually wobbled. Was I really this unhinged?

An unfortunate high-pitched giggle interrupted my thoughts. When I realized it was coming from me, I covered my mouth. Fantastic. So much for making a great impression. With Brad closing the space between us one long stride at a time, I quickly employed Virginia's breathing technique, and while my pulse still sprinted, I managed to stop the obnoxious sounds.

"Zoe, welcome to Georgia." Brad held out his arms, and before I could say Feng Shui, he enveloped me in a hug. Unable to stand on my own strength, I fell into his firm chest.

I might have stayed in his arms a little longer than would be considered normal, but I didn't know if there was a protocol for hugging a co-worker. Actually, most people would probably consider it sexual harassment, but it wasn't like that. It was so warm and friendly, and bonus, it gave me time to gather my senses because stars were zipping around my head like I was a cartoon character who'd just been punched.

"Thank you. I'm glad to be here," I said as we moved apart. *Good girl, Zoe. You sounded totally normal.*

He surveyed the area behind me. "Where's Wren?"

And if I needed more to remind me who H.B. preferred and how *friendly* his hug was, I had it. A rush of anxiety heated my skin. I fanned my face. "After her grandmother's funeral, Wren decided she needed to stay in Chicago and help her parents. I thought Megan told you."

"No." His brows bunched together with as much concern as I was feeling. But he didn't know that—or was my anxiety so evident that he could sense it?

"Well, Wren will be here for a quick visit next week, but it's pretty much going to be you and me. I hope that's okay." I bounced on my toes, smiling in a way I hoped expressed confidence.

"It doesn't seem like I have a choice." He studied me as if I were an alien. He wasn't frowning like he was upset, but I spotted his jaw twitch like he was grinding his molars.

"I'm sorry." I let the corners of my lips fall. It apparently wasn't improving anything anyway, but of course once my guard was down, a stupid giggle escaped.

Brad's eyes grew wide. "Is something funny?"

"No, sorry. Nervous habit." And again, I was bouncing.

"Right, sorry, I didn't mean to stress you out. It's just that I need this project to be perfect. Y'all are a great team, but Wren always seemed to call the shots."

"I assure you we have the same goal. I promise I'll do everything I can to have a positive outcome. Working together, I'm sure we'll have amazing results." Wow, I was even convincing myself, although I'm relatively sure I was just quoting something Virginia told me during the flight.

"Okay." His gaze shifted to my leg, where apparently my hand had decided to tap out a rapid rhythm. I balled my fist. Well, at least I'd sounded professional and stopped talking before I exclaimed *that teamwork makes the dream work*. And in my defense, Brad had never seemed this intense on our video meetings. Something else seemed to be bothering him, or at least I hoped I wasn't that annoying.

Brad hooked a thumb over his shoulder. "Let's get your luggage, and on the way to the development, we can discuss our first problem and how we can solve it."

Chapter Two

♥

In the stillness of the morning, I heard the rumble of Brad's truck arriving at the property. Our clients, Fred and Linda, had insisted that we use the guest cottage while we oversaw the renovations. The only other accommodations were an hour away in Savannah or at the bed-and-breakfast twenty minutes away in the small town of Haslemere.

The house was part of a development that'd been abandoned years ago. Not only was the design out of date, but it'd been built with subpar materials. Brad and his crew had already demoed the kitchen and bathrooms, and we'd ordered new energy-efficient windows and exterior doors. While we completed the renovation, we'd also be working with an architect to finalize plans for a clubhouse and with a landscape designer on creating a place that would help the potential homeowners see Magnolia Bluff as a place to unwind from their busy lives. It was a tremendous investment for Linda and Fred, but as we drove through the development, I could see why they'd chosen it. If everything went as planned, it'd be a slice of heaven on earth.

Before I'd gone to bed, I'd made sure the oven worked and was hoping that after we dealt with our current problem, Brad would drive me to a grocery store. I needed to buy supplies for stress baking. The first thing I'd make was a batch of the muffins that Brad's mom had sent, but I needed the recipe. I'd asked for it, but he claimed that some of his Nana's recipes were considered family secrets.

I slipped into my metallic teal wedge sandals with the adorable tulle bow that perched on top. They matched my headband and belt perfectly. I wanted to look my best for our meeting, and maybe for Brad too. Together we could resolve the issue with the grumpy neighbor and stay on schedule with the renovations.

I found a lot of comfort in the word *we*, especially when the *we* was in reference to Brad and me. For whatever delusional reason, I knew that *we* were better together than apart. But even more than the *we* that was Brad and me were all the times when a person I was helping achieved a goal. I'd never cared much about winning anything for myself, but I got a lot of satisfaction from helping others succeed.

And after I'd received Wren's text while I was unpacking the night before, I felt confident that this project would be a win for all of us.

With the bounce back in my step and a twinkle in my eyes, or at least I hoped my shimmery rose eye shadow would achieve that effect, I left the cottage and met Brad in the drive. "Good morning."

As his gaze landed on me, his brows inched up. "Do you always sparkle?" It didn't sound like a compliment, but he spared me that swoon-worthy lopsided grin.

"If I can help it. My favorite art teacher in high school kept a sign above her door that said, 'never let anyone dull your sparkle'. I suppose I kind of made it my personal mission in life."

"Interesting. I think it's only supposed to be a metaphor."

"Sure, but living it literally is so much more fun."

"I totally see that, but I'm not sure our grumpy neighbor will agree. You might want to tone it down a little." Brad pulled a navy blazer from his truck and slipped it on. "Look, I'm not a fan of formal wear, but I'm making the sacrifice."

My gut twisted with his words, bringing to the surface unpleasant memories, but it wasn't like he wasn't also changing his style for the meeting. "I guess I can do without the belt and headband." I started back to the cottage.

"Losing a couple accessories doesn't dull your personality." He fell in step beside me. "By the way, I'm sorry if I was a little distracted last night."

"That's a bit of an understatement, but I accept your apology."

"Wow, don't hold back. I guess all this sparkle requires a lot of charge. I don't remember you being so feisty on our video calls."

Because I'd always deferred to Wren, which was fine, but he'd struck a nerve asking me to change. And I kind of felt like he owed me a better explanation. And maybe I could get that recipe if I played my cards right. "So where was Mr. Charming?"

"You think I'm charming?"

"Seriously? You know you normally add an extra dose of Southern swagger to our conversations."

He chuckled. "All right, I confess. I learned at a young age that a smile and talking with a Southern drawl can be very persuasive."

"I bet it got you out of all kinds of trouble."

"Now, why would you think I'd be any trouble?"

"I think that says it all." I opened the door to the cottage and tossed my belt and headband on the chair inside. "And you still haven't answered my question. Is there more bad news, or is the neighbor the only problem?"

On the drive from the airport, Brad told me that on the first day of demo, the man who lived in the only other house on the bluff right next to the reno house had stormed over and demanded an explanation from the supervisor. Brad hadn't been on site, and since the design firm was technically overseeing the project, he wanted to wait for Wren and me before approaching the neighbor.

"I guess I was also caught off guard when Wren wasn't with you. Not that I don't think you aren't up to the job, but she seemed more—"

Not wanting him to confirm his doubts about me, I held up a hand as I shut the door. "I have some good news. I can't believe I forgot to mention it right away."

"Zoe, I didn't mean—"

"No, no." I waved away his concern. "It's fine. I've never sought the spotlight or vied for a leadership position. It just isn't my thing, so when Wren texted that she's coming and staying, I was as relieved as I'm sure you probably are right now."

"Really? She's coming? When?"

"A couple of days, I think. We didn't get into the details."

"So, should we put off this meeting?" Brad pointed at the neighbor's house, which I had to admit was objectively stunning. The exterior featured weathered grey cedar shingles that were perfectly accented by simple white porch posts and black shutters.

"I don't think so, but I'm happy to let you take the lead with him."

"All right. Let's do this." He headed across the lawn. "But Zoe, don't think for one second I don't think you could handle the neighbor or the project."

As I hurried to keep up with his long legs, I tripped on the uneven terrain and grabbed onto the crook of his arm for balance. "Not even a second, huh?"

"Okay, maybe you seemed a little nervous last night." He held my hand in place. "And maybe your ways are unconventional, but I never doubted that you'd do whatever it took to help me succeed. To be honest, that's what I needed to hear most last night."

"And why was that?"

"That's a story for another day. Suffice it to say, I want to take over the family company, but first I need to prove to my dad that I'm ready."

"And this is just the project to do it. Got it."

We stepped onto the porch, and Brad pressed the doorbell. After a few moments, a man who might have been attractive, if not for his scowl, opened the door.

"Good morning, sir. I'm Brad Chastain with Chastain Construction, and this is Zoe Stockton with the Bespoke Design Firm from Chicago." Brad held out his hand. "We hope we can clear up any misunderstandings and assure you of the scope of the project. We certainly didn't intend to cause you any problems and want to do everything we can to ease your concerns." Brad gave a reassuring smile.

This guy might not find solace in his words, but I found myself gaping at Brad as all kinds of warm fuzzies filled me.

Stop it, Zoe! He isn't interested! This is work!

"There's nothing you can say." But the man grasped Brad's hand. Apparently, in the South, you still shook even as you sneered. "I've already called my own contractor about constructing a wall around my property, and I'll be planting a large hedge."

"But, sir." Brad gestured to the property line, the vein on his neck pulsing. "You can't—"

"I *what*—"

"Mr. Chastain simply means is that if you'll allow us, we can show you the landscape design, which is meant to provide peace—"

"I'll take care of my peace." His glare zeroed in on me.

I retreated, rolling my lips between my teeth.

"Now, I'm not sure how you were brought up—" Brad shifted between me and the man—"but that's not how you speak to a lady, and I'd appreciate you showing Miss Stockton some respect."

"And I'd appreciate you getting off my porch and staying off my property." He poked Brad in his chest.

Brad clenched his fist at his side, and before he could land what I'm sure would have been a very satisfactory punch to the man's face,

I grabbed Brad's hand. "Let's go. He's not worth it. Remember your future."

"Best you listen to the sprite." The man pivoted toward the door.

Brad tensed. "I should—"

"Nope. We're leaving." I guided him down the stairs. "I recently learned a breathing trick. Inhale with me and hold your breath while you count to three." Surprisingly, Brad followed my instructions as we proceeded across the driveway. Once we made it to the back of the reno house, I didn't need to hold his hand. But he didn't pull away from me, so I held on for another moment as the tension drifted away and lovely little tingles skipped over my skin. "So, that didn't go as well as I'd hoped."

"What a total—" He clamped his mouth shut. "Sorry, I was about to call him something, but I was raised right, so I won't." He sighed, shoulders slumping.

Unable to watch his confidence wane, I quirked a brow, grinning. "How about a total moose?"

He checked my expression, as if he was making sure he'd heard me correctly, and then nodded. "Why a moose? They seem pretty chill. What about a fried tarantula?"

"Or a boiled cockroach," I squeaked out between giggles.

Laughing, Brad released my hand and pushed his fingers through his hair. "Not that this hasn't been fun, but what are we going to tell Wren?"

"That we dressed professionally, and it didn't work." I shot him a look. It wasn't entirely his fault, but I knew better than to change for anyone, and I wouldn't do it again, even for Brad.

He winced. "Point taken. Sorry. But seriously, he cannot build a wall."

At least Brad showed some remorse, and I could get Nana's recipe after all. "Don't worry. I'll bake some muffins for Wren to take with her. It'll be fine. She's used to dealing with troublesome people. You should meet her mom."

"I hope you're right."

"I am." I smiled sweetly, batting my lashes. "And you know the best muffin I've had in a long time was your mom's, so do you think you could get me the recipe?"

"Nicely played, Stockton. I'll see what I can do. In the meantime, how about a tour of the progress?" As his gaze met mine, he smiled, and not the charming one or the flirty one, but one that was warm and genuine, and my insides softened like butter for cookies. I wanted to see that expression more.

Chapter Three

♥

Almost three weeks later

When Wren arrived two weeks ago, she'd declared a "no drama zone" around the project. But since a "no drama zone" didn't apply to the clients, Linda decided to throw a reveal party for a few potential buyers, even though the renovations wouldn't be complete. Apparently, she'd consulted the shared spreadsheet and believed we'd be ready. With one week already gone since Linda's initial email, she'd arranged a video call with all of us and the architect, Jared, who lived near Charleston.

Now, Brad, Wren, and I gathered in the kitchen around a piece of plywood that, if everything stayed on schedule, would be replaced by a slab of Carrera marble before the party that was in only fourteen days and approximately thirty hours. But who was counting?

While Wren's *no-drama zone* was initially only regarding deliveries being on time and correct, it'd taken on a different meaning when she'd confronted the grumpy neighbor. In a twist that proved life is in fact stranger than fiction, the man next door turned out to be Nathaniel Sullivan, Wren's favorite author.

Over the weeks since their meeting, they'd formed a friendship that was zinging with so many sparks that it didn't seem unlikely they might set the house on fire. Of course, Wren claimed he was only helping her fulfill the challenges her grandmother had made a requirement in her will for her inheritance. Meanwhile, Nathaniel claimed he was keeping an eye on the person in charge of the project. Remarkably, once Wren tamed the beast, Nathaniel was okay and so sweet to Wren, like butter-cream-frosting-sweet.

Unfortunately for Brad, it meant that Wren wasn't going to be more than a friend. When I'd mentioned I might be interested in a little reno romance with our general contractor, she'd asked me to let her talk to him first. I'd totally agreed with her because *no drama*, and I wasn't in the market for anything serious. Just dinner out with a guy that I might be attracted to, but really, most women would be attracted to Brad, so casually dating him didn't seem like an opportunity to be missed. But that was on Monday, and now it was Friday, and we'd been too busy for anyone to have a conversation about anything other than work and party planning.

While I appreciated that Wren was simultaneously falling in love and rediscovering her inner artist, it'd come with *more* drama because she'd completely redesigned the clubhouse for the development. If it hadn't been so unbelievably inspired, I'd have groaned about it and even questioned our ability to pull it off. Instead, I encouraged her. Because while I love to see people reach their goals, when I can help them achieve their dreams, my proverbial cup overflows.

At least when Linda had requested we arrange for some light hors d'oeuvres and drinks to be served, my initial bout of panic was cured by enlisting the help of Bonnie, Nathaniel's housekeeper. As a self-declared follower, I'd developed a keen sense of who were take-charge kinds of people, and Bonnie absolutely fit the mold. Not to mention, she was a fantastic cook—win, win.

I set up my tablet so we could all be seen. "We have about five minutes."

"Are we still good to pick up the planters and artwork after we finish?" Brad removed his baseball hat.

As he leaned against the makeshift counter, I caught his delightful scent, warm and woodsy, but not too musky, with a subtle crispness. And I held my breath for a moment as tiny thrills twirled through me. "Yes, and do you have any time tomorrow? I know it's Saturday, but I might need help getting the swings if they can't deliver them. They're having trouble with their truck."

Wren needed to hurry up with that friend talk, especially if Brad and I were going to be spending time alone together in the cab of his truck. But what if he wasn't interested? Over the last three weeks, I'd sensed something more, but he'd pursued Wren, which would've been fine with me. Except the way she described the relationship, it didn't sound like they had any chemistry.

With the scientific theory in mind, I met his gaze and held it, testing my hypothesis. If my experiment had been on what happens when a force of attraction draws two particles together, then the result would've been that time and space stand still and fade into nothingness. The results were a strange sensation. One that was both gripping all my nerves and making them shiver. But what made my experiment the most interesting was Brad's mirrored reaction.

Then, with what can only be described as a jolt of awareness, Brad shook his head, nearly jumping backward, like the energy pulsing between us had reached the maximum and shot him away. "Just let me know." He turned his attention to Wren. So much for keeping the drama to a minimum.

Wren's brows pinched together as she pressed her fingers into her shoulders.

"Let me." Brad stepped behind her and massaged her shoulders. At first, her eyes went round with surprise, but I could tell that Brad knew what he was doing by the way Wren didn't even bother to protest, and I couldn't blame her.

But I could be frustrated with Brad. What was his deal? First, he'd stared into my eyes with ardent attraction, and then he'd acted like I burned him and concentrated on giving Wren what appeared to be an expert massage.

"Might want to wrap it up." I pointed at the screen, trying to ignore the burning in my chest. I had no reason to be jealous. We were all friends, and friends did nice things for each other, and like Wren said, it wasn't worth the drama. "Linda and Fred are connecting."

"Right." Wren patted Brad's hand. "Thanks."

"Hello, all. Thanks again for being so flexible." Fred shot Linda a stink eye. "Some people have bigger dreams than time allows for."

Wren tucked a lock of hair behind her ear. "We're happy to make them come true."

"Ha, to be honest, I didn't even know to dream this way. Wren and Zoe, you've done amazing work," Linda said, as Jared joined the meeting. "Jared, I reviewed the new clubhouse designs, and I think they're perfect. We'll want renderings for the party."

"Yes, ma'am. I'm glad you like them."

"What about the landscape?" Fred asked.

"The roads and entry have been cleaned up and new plants installed. We'll have the landscape architect complete a design with the new building plans and send them to you as soon as possible." Wren jotted a note.

"We need some examples of the plants on display at our house. I assume they'll be similar, but if not, we need photos," Linda said.

"We'll take care of it," Wren said.

I leaned in front of the camera. "Have you reviewed the menu?"

"Yes, I think it'll be perfect. Please have Bonnie send us an invoice for her services and any expenses, and let's be sure to ask that neighbor. You said he's her boss."

"I'm sure Wren can manage that." I wiggled my brows at her.

It was a harmless joke, and no one else would've caught the insinuation, but Wren's skin looked like someone had doused her with red paint.

"I'll invite him, but I can't promise he'll come," she said with an amazing amount of poise, given that her face was ablaze.

Fred's brows bunched. "Is he still reticent about the development?"

"He certainly won't be rolling out a welcome mat." Brad's nostrils flared. Apparently, he still hadn't gotten over our initial meetings with Nathaniel. In his defense, Wren said that Nathaniel continued to refer to Brad as the oaf.

Like the consummate professional she was, Wren squared her shoulders and focused on the tiny camera. "Nathaniel is coming around to the idea. He's actually an author and was just worried about his peace and quiet. I'm doing everything I can think of to reassure him."

Giggles tickled the corners of my lips, but with a great deal of effort, I maintained a professional expression. It might be hilarious later when I'd definitely be teasing Wren, but right now, I had to hold it together.

Thankfully, Fred and Linda were reviewing something in front of them, oblivious to the very opposite of a non-drama scene happening on our side of the camera.

"Fine, fine. We'll do whatever you think to get him on board." Linda checked with Fred before she directed her attention to the rest of us. "And now we have some exciting news." She clapped.

Wren glanced at me with wide eyes. Just because Linda was applauding didn't mean it was good news for us. It could just as easily be a lot more work to do with no time.

"One of our guests is Cheryl Tolleson, a producer for the Living Well Network. She's very interested in our project both for personal and professional reasons," Linda said.

While Wren stared at the screen, gaping, I bounced on my toes. "That's really exciting."

Finally schooling her expression, Wren asked, "When you say, 'personal and professional reasons,' what does that mean?"

"Exactly what it sounds like. Cheryl and her husband are hunting for a place to build a home to rest and recharge. When I told her about the location and showed her your new designs with all the local craftspeople and artists, she was intrigued." Linda shrugged. "It might amount to nothing beyond a new client, but I wanted you to know you are likely also pitching a television show."

"And we will be ready." Wren nodded. "Thanks so much for this opportunity."

"Wonderful. Chat soon." Linda waved.

"Keep up the good work." Fred reached forward, and their screen went dark.

"Good to see y'all. Let me know if you need anything," Jared, who I'd almost forgotten was on the call, said before he left.

Wren turned to Brad and me. "So that was unexpected."

"Yeah, you did a great job of hiding your shock." I finally let the giggles free.

Brad chuckled. "I thought you were going to faint." He hugged Wren to his side.

Scrunching up her nose like she'd inhaled a harsh chemical, Wren shifted out of his embrace. "Well, I guess we better get back to work, but let's keep each other updated on any setbacks as quickly as possible." She gathered her things and hurried out of the house.

"Is she okay?" Brad's forehead creased with concern.

"I think so. She's just worried about getting everything completed."

"Right. Well, I guess we need to get going." He avoided my eyes as he put on his ball cap. "We have a lot of stops to make."

I nudged his arm. "Hey, I know how important the success of this project is for you, and I promise I won't let anything mess it up. I'm on your team."

"Thanks." He spared me that perfect smile. "How 'bout I take you to one of my favorite lunch spots?"

Chapter Four

Fear can really warp a person's perspective, and the more time I spent with Brad, the more I wondered what was motivating him. Something about our conversation with Linda and Fred had him withdrawing, or was it Wren's unexplained and sudden departure? I'd ask her about that later, but since Brad and I were spending the rest of the day together, I wanted to ease his concerns.

Although I was ready for Wren to tell Brad they'd only be friends, since she hadn't, Brad and I could talk as friends without the pressure of romance.

But first I quietly went through Virginia's breathing exercises to extinguish the sparkler candles still flickering with excitement inside me. I'd seen a less serious side of Brad, but when he was in this state, my enthusiasm seemed to get under his skin. As we drove out of the development, Brad focused on the road, frowning and shaking his head, like he was trying to solve a difficult problem and couldn't find the right strategy.

I'd make it my mission today to help him relax and even have a little fun. He certainly knew he didn't need to be serious with me.

With my nerves almost in check, I slowly exhaled. "So, it's a pretty huge deal that Cheryl Tolleson is going to be at the party. I told Wren that Linda and Fred's connections could lead to something like this. Can you believe you might be the star of your own show?"

"That's never going to happen." He gripped the steering wheel tighter.

Okay, definitely not the reaction I expected, but I continued, "If everything goes well, it sounded like a possibility."

"Not for me and not for Chastain Construction. That's not our scene. My dad would be horrified by the mere mention of it. One time my mom showed Dad a renovation show, and he hated it."

"Yikes. Hate's a strong word. What was the problem?"

"In his words, unrealistic expectations."

"I guess I can see his point, but—"

"No, absolutely no buts. Dad pointed out everything they did wrong, how it wouldn't work in the end, how they were wasting money. He went on and on about how our clients would expect us to do those things. I'm telling you, it is not an option." Brad smacked the blinker so hard I was afraid the switchy thing might snap off.

"Got it." I threw my hands up in surrender.

Brad glanced at me. "Sorry. It's just I'm under a lot of pressure."

"From your dad?"

"Yes and no. I'm ready to take over the business, but he's still micromanaging me." Brad white-knuckled the steering wheel. "It doesn't matter. I'll worry about the TV show if it ever becomes a reality. Until then, we have plenty to do."

"You're right." I shifted my attention to the pine trees lined up in rows along the road. Sunlight poured through the high branches covered in needles, letting the warm glow play with the thin shadows. The enchanted scene served as a beautiful distraction from my disappointment. I couldn't imagine giving up the chance to be on one of the Living Well Network's shows. Maybe Brad's priorities would change once he was in charge of Chastain Construction, but we still needed to make that happen.

"Thanks for understanding and for working so hard on everything. You and Wren have been great. If we can get the porch swings this afternoon, I can hang them."

"And we'll be ahead of schedule."

"Exactly but don't tell Linda. I don't want to give her any ideas that she can add more assignments before the party."

"So true."

Brad parked the car in front of a small house with a large storage building to the side. The words on the side of the building read, *Everything Plants But the Plants*. "How did y'all know about this place?"

"Wren went to the market in Haslemere and made a lot of connections. She returned with a stack of business cards. We've been researching the local craftspeople and how we could implement their work in our designs. It's really been inspiring."

"I still can't believe y'all changed the entire plan for the clubhouse."

"Neither can I. It was very un-Wren-like, but it's going to be gorgeous and look like it's always been on the property."

"I'm glad I get to create with y'all and experience the design side of the construction process. I'm always just implementing the plans, behind the scenes."

"Your ideas about materials and the spaces have been invaluable."

A slight blush colored his cheeks. "Thanks. Ready?" He exited the cab.

I don't know whose shadow you've been hiding in, Brad Chastain, but I'm about to help you emerge and shine.

I dashed after him. "Hey, wait up. You do realize that I have to take four steps for every one of yours."

"I thought with all that fairy glitter you could simply raise your wings and fly."

"If only I had a wand." I twirled in front of him. "What would your wish be, Mr. Chastain?"

"Don't be silly, Zoe."

"Why not? You know, it's okay to loosen up. It might even help you be more successful." I stopped in front of him and held up my finger like it was a fairy wand. "So tell me. What's that secret something that you really want?"

"I don't need anything."

"I didn't ask what you needed. What do you want? Come on, it can be totally impractical. As a matter of fact, it should be." I rose on my toes and tapped my finger on his shoulder.

Brad clasped my hand and spun me under his arm. "Right now, I wish we could get these planter boxes, so we could get some lunch, and if that means dancing you to the door, I'm game." He placed his other hand on my waist, holding me close.

My breath caught in my chest as heat pooled in my belly.

We didn't move for a moment. Normally, this kind of situation would send me into a fit of giggles, but perhaps without oxygen, it was impossible. I gasped, and my breaths came hard and fast, like we actually had been dancing.

And then the best sound echoed around me—Brad's laughter. He dipped me dramatically before standing me on my feet and turning me to the door of the warehouse. "You, Miss Stockton, are too much."

"Nice moves, Mr. Chastain. I didn't know you had it in you."

"You shouldn't underestimate me."

"Never again." My words came out all breathy and deep instead of flirty and light. I swallowed, clearing my throat. "By the way, I wasn't so distracted that I didn't realize you failed to tell me your wish."

"True, but it seems we've made it to our destination." Brad held the door. "After you."

"Thank you, but you can't charm your way around answering forever."

"I always like a challenge."

"Me too." But I dropped it because I didn't want to push him too hard and have him clam up on me. Since we were keeping things strictly in the friend zone, we'd have lots more time to talk. And right now, I was loving peeling away each layer of Brad, revealing new and interesting things about this man. I

After we loaded the custom planter boxes in the bed of Brad's truck, we stopped at a gas station that Brad swore sold some of the best barbecue in Georgia from their lunch counter. Then Brad drove to a bluff overlooking a wide river. Wren had told me Brad had an eye for beautiful scenery, and he didn't disappoint.

A sprawling oak tree arched its branches, creating shade from the hot rays of the afternoon sun. After Brad lowered the truck's tailgate, we sat on it and unpacked our food. Dark river water, the color of coffee, drifted by the bright green grasses that rustled along the banks.

"This is so peaceful." I took a bite of my pulled pork sandwich.

Brad pointed a battered fry at me. "Let's keep it that way."

"You're no fun."

"I'm loads of fun, but—"

"There's always a but with you, and I totally get it. We're all under a lot of pressure, but promise me when this is over, and you're a huge success, and your dad passes over the reins, you'll take a day off and enjoy something you love."

"Promise." He gazed over the scene, chewing his food.

"What would that look like?"

"Hmm. I've been wanting to go deep sea fishing. How about you?" He lifted his sandwich to his mouth.

"I'd love to spend a whole day exploring antique stores around the area. While searching for pieces we can use, I've seen so many interesting places online. I love all things vintage. It's always been a passion of mine, searching through stores for interesting and lovely items. They all tell a story."

"You could stay busy for a week, maybe longer. I swear there's an antique shop on two corners in every town in Georgia."

"Hopefully, we'll get to visit a few before we finish this installation."

"I'll ask my mom for suggestions." He swallowed the last of his sandwich and folded the paper into a square. "I hate to eat and run, but if we want to make it to the gallery and the swing shop before it closes, we need to get a move on."

"Okay. I'm too full to finish, but I'm saving this for later." I carefully wrapped the parchment around my sandwich. "You were right. It was delicious."

"Glad you liked it, and lucky for you, I keep a small cooler in the cab for leftovers." Brad cleaned up the trash and closed the tailgate.

After one last glance at the river, I absorbed the scenery along the road as we drove to the gallery and collected several pieces of art made entirely of oyster shells. Then, we headed to the porch swing shop that was almost an hour away, but we arrived with fifteen minutes to spare and loaded the swings. With the sun setting in front of us, we returned to the reno house and unloaded everything in the garage.

"Looks like Wren's already turned in for the night." I gestured to the darkened cottage. It'd been such a lovely day, and I wasn't ready for it to end. Brad and I might never be more than friends, which was okay. I enjoyed his company, and romance complicated everything. The last thing I wanted to do was make things more difficult for Brad.

"It's still pretty early." Beside his truck, Brad rocked on his heels. "If you don't have any plans, we could get something from the General's Diner in Haslemere. Have you been yet?"

"Not to the diner, but Wren gushed over their peach milkshakes, and my only plans tonight were to attempt to stream a movie and eat my leftover sandwich."

"I mean, I hate for you to miss out on that."

"Ha ha. Let's check out the diner, but it's my treat."

"I'm not going to fight you for it." He opened the passenger door.

Once we arrived in the small town of Haslemere, we strolled to the diner. It was an adorable town with a historic town hall in the center, surrounded by ancient trees and a gazebo on the corner. Around the square, quaint shops lined the quiet streets, like a movie set.

We claimed a booth and ordered the dinner special and milkshakes. Over our meal, we discussed our favorite movies and places we'd like to visit. Brad told me about the first fish he'd caught and some of the mischief he'd gotten into as a kid. I was surprised that this mostly serious guy had been a bit of a troublemaker growing up.

I shared with him how I'd taught myself to bake through a lot of mistakes because while I'd learned the importance of measuring, in the beginning, it seemed like it took away from the creativity. He laughed but also offered to eat any results of my stress baking. And I promised I kept my creativity to decorations these days.

After what seemed like no time, I realized our table was clean and we were the last diners in the restaurant. "I guess they'd probably like us to go."

Brad checked his watch. "I can't believe we've been here this long." He stood and held out his hand. "Ready?"

I took it and rose, but not wanting to change our dynamics, I released his hand as we left the diner. Unfortunately, the damage was done, and an awkward tension hummed between us in the silence of the truck. Our conversation had been so easy, and even when we touched, it'd seemed natural—until it'd felt extra. We simply needed a neutral topic to get us back on track.

"So do you have any siblings?" I asked.

"Just my sister, Carleigh. She's a bigwig lobbyist in DC." His voice held an edge, and I wished I'd chosen the weather instead.

"I have four siblings, and I'm right in the middle," I said, hoping he'd offer something else. Most people at least gave me a sympathetic groan when they heard my place in the birth order, but Brad said nothing. What was the deal with his sister?

I didn't bother trying another topic, and after a few minutes, Brad switched on the radio. When we arrived at the house, I thanked him for hanging out and jumped out of the cab.

"It was fun." He waved. "See you in the morning."

With that, he was gone.

And my insides were tied in knots that I didn't understand. Maybe I'd whip up some scones or cinnamon rolls. If I baked late into the night, I might be able to get some sleep.

Chapter Five

♥

Usually baking alleviated my stress, and if that didn't work, eating the results completed the job. But when I woke on Saturday and found a text from Brad explaining that he would need to put off hanging the swings until later, no amount of sugary carbohydrates could relieve my anxiety. Not that I didn't try. But after devouring a couple of cinnamon rolls and too many scones to count, I was left with my stomach not only still tied in knots but also filled with what felt like a concrete garden orb.

After my ineffective pastry treatment, I went for a long walk where I attempted to convince myself that Brad wasn't avoiding me. And when that didn't work, I curled up on my bed for an Emma Stone marathon. Thankfully, between the copious amount of calories I'd consumed, I dozed off early and woke up Sunday morning to my phone chiming with incoming texts.

Brad: Good morning.

Brad: Sorry about bailing yesterday. Family stuff. But I'm available after church.

I rubbed my eyes and re-read the messages. So I had overreacted.

Me: No worries. What time should I expect you?

Brad: 11??

Me: See you then. I'll pay you in muffins.

Brad: Even better.

I checked the time. *Fantastic*. I had almost three hours to endure before he'd arrive, and I'd used up all my flour on Friday night. I smothered my face with a pillow.

Why was it so hard just being friends with Brad? Since my toxic relationship in college, I'd had no trouble casually dating. But something happened during my time with Brad on Friday. In some ways our conversations felt so intimate, and it seemed like we were on the brink of getting deep. Did I want that? Why not? Sharing what was important in our lives grew friendships, and Brad and I were friends, so it was totally natural, even expected.

And if I kept repeating that to myself, everything would be fine, and I'd be able to keep my feelings in check.

One exceptionally long shower, a healthy breakfast with actual fruit, and a lot of social media scrolling later, the rumble of Brad's truck finally broke the silence. I sprang from the couch and strolled—okay, sort of jogged—to the front of the house. As Brad rounded the truck, I waited, knowing exactly when I'd learn if things between us were cool.

"Hey, there." Brad tossed an arm around my shoulders and squeezed me to his side.

Thank goodness. We were still on hugging terms, and Brad hugged everyone he considered a friend.

"Hey." I returned the embrace before we strolled to the garage. "Thanks for working on a Sunday."

"I don't consider hanging swings work, but to be sure, we'll enjoy them once they're up."

"Sounds good. Just tell me how I can help."

"Let's move them both to the yard, and then we'll get the chains, tools, and ladder."

"Ready when you are." I grasped under the seat at one end of the swing. While they weren't too heavy for Brad, because of the length, they required two people to carry them.

Brad lifted with me. "I'll walk backwards."

"Okay." We crossed the yard. "How was church? I try to watch my home church online, but the service out here is terrible."

"It was fine. I went to my parents' for brunch. We usually have a big lunch, but my sister is going to be on Sea Island for the night. She has important meetings this week, so my parents are driving down there to have supper with her. Apparently, it's the only time she can squeeze them in."

"You didn't want to go?"

"We have too much work here, and they won't be back until after lunch tomorrow." He stopped beneath one of the frames, and we lowered the swing.

"Brad, we could've managed for half a day."

"It's fine. By the way, I talked to my mom about furniture shops, and we might need to check out this one place." He turned for the garage. "I'll show you the website when we finish."

"Okay. I just hate that you don't see your sister often and you're missing this chance."

"We'll catch up some other time. Do you see your family a lot?"

"My mom tries to host family dinners a few times a year, but it's hard to get all of us together. My older sister and brother both have kids and live in the suburbs, but I try to meet up with the twins at least once a month." I positioned myself to carry the other swing.

"You didn't mention they were twins." As we exited the garage, Brad pulled a face. The one I'd been expecting on Friday night.

"Yep."

"So what was that like? Growing up with all those siblings."

"Fine. It made me good at working with people and compromise. I'm not at all competitive, so I never experienced sibling rivalry. I was happy to cheer them all on."

"And you're still doing that," he said as we placed the swing on the ground and returned to the garage.

"So how about you? Did you and your sister get along?"

"Most of the time. She's a couple of years older than me and the typical overachiever, not to mention super smart and talented and never got in trouble."

"Come on. No one's that perfect. You make her sound like some kind of saint."

He grabbed a ladder and his toolbox. "My parents certainly see her that way. And to be fair, Carleigh's earned everything she's achieved. It's not her fault I was such a menace in high school." But surely, his parents knew he was great at his job and loyal to them and their business.

With the box of chains, I followed him across the yard. "You certainly aren't a menace now. We couldn't have pulled this off without your help."

"Thanks," he said, but when his cheeks reddened, I focused on hanging the swings.

Once Brad had checked the chains were secure, we sat together. With the breeze off the river and the shade of the trees, it was the perfect conditions for a nap. Instead, sitting so close to Brad had my adrenaline keeping me very much awake.

"Hey, weren't you going to show me a furniture website?"

"Right." Brad scrolled through his phone. "This woman works with a small team of craftspeople. They find old furniture and other items and either restore them or make something entirely different with them, like lamps and chandeliers."

"Oh, wow, this chest is gorgeous." I tapped the screen, enlarging the picture.

"She has a YouTube channel. Everything's time lapsed, so you can see the entire process."

"Can we watch one?"

"Yeah, but fair warning, it's addictive. I completely lost track of time last night, watching them."

"Now I have to see one." I selected the icon as he shifted closer, his shoulder meeting mine.

After the video ended, I glanced at him, our gazes colliding. "One more?" I'm not sure how friction works in an empty space, but I do know that the air between us was sparking enough to start a fire.

"I warned you." He stared into my eyes for another beat, but then dropped his focus. "I better get this stuff cleaned up." He gave me a quick side hug and stood.

"Hi, there." Wren crossed the lawn. "The swings look fantastic."

"Hi." I hopped up, my cheeks heating. "Brad was such a sweetheart and offered to hang them today after church."

"Thanks, Brad." The corner of Wren's lip quirked up, like she doubted the innocence of our circumstances.

"Uh, it, uh, was no problem." As he peered at us, red splotches crept up his neck. "All part of the job. I was just heading out."

"I promised him payment in muffins," I blurted, fully aware Wren was eyeing me like she'd caught me licking batter off a spoon.

"Brad, you've gone above and beyond. We'll be sure to let Linda and Fred know," Wren said.

"Do you want to try it out?" I gestured to the swing. "I'll grab those muffins." I gave Brad what I hoped was an encouraging smile before I turned and hurried to the cottage. How would he take it when Wren told him she only wanted to be friends?

Inside, I grabbed a basket and tossed in a half dozen muffins. Surely, he was feeling the attraction between us. If his red skin was any indication, at the very least he was having more than friendly feelings for me and felt guilty since he'd been seeing Wren.

Regardless, we'd connected on so many levels, and I wouldn't give up our friendship. I just might want more. I left the cottage and crossed the lawn as Wren left Brad on the swing.

She stopped in front of me, grinning. "Let H.B. out of the friend zone. We're cool."

"You're sure?"

"Of course. Have fun." She strode past me.

"Here you go." I held up the basket to Brad. "I'm sorry you have to leave."

He rose, studying me like he was seeing me for the first time. "It's probably for the best."

"Oh, okay." I twisted my lips to stop them from frowning, but it didn't stop the disappointment dipping inside me.

He glanced at the muffins and then the garage and then back to me. "Actually, we could hang the party lights, if you don't mind helping me out a little longer."

"Sure." I shifted my attention to the basket. "Want a snack?"

Logically, we all understood that a minute is always sixty seconds, an hour sixty minutes, and a day twenty-four hours, but every one of those seconds seemed to zip by faster and faster as the days leading up to the reveal party grew closer. We needed every project to stay on schedule, and currently, the muralist whom we'd hired to create a statement wall in the dining room was MIA.

Thankfully, Brad's mom's suggestion for the reclaimed furniture and lighting was spot on, and the mantel builder Wren and I'd discovered had two examples of his craftsmanship in his workshop that he was willing to loan us for the party. After a debriefing and making sure the subs knew what needed to be completed, Brad and I'd left Wren to supervise the work at the reno house. We'd decided it was most efficient for Brad and me to go together to collect sample items from suppliers. We could also source any new items to use at the clubhouse and to add to the décor of Fred and Linda's house. Brad knew where the shops were located and the fastest way to get to them, and I knew the design aesthetic.

It might have been all work, but I couldn't deny it was a perk spending the day exploring with Brad. Between stops, we talked about everything and nothing, and while he seemed to be making an extra effort not to touch me or flirt, we were growing closer in that intimate way that I was pretty sure would not end well. Our conversation was so natural that I found myself sharing more than I normally did, and I got the impression he was doing the same.

After we left the last business on our list, he suggested we stop for supper. I don't know why, but when he used the word supper, it warmed my soul with something that felt like home. In the same part of my brain that understood the basic math of seconds and minutes, his practical invitation to share a meal morphed into a romantic rendezvous that I certainly wasn't turning down, even if it was completely innocent.

With our plans set, I sent Wren a text updating her, then put my phone away, determined to enjoy my circumstances. "Do I get to experience another hidden gem tonight?"

"Maybe." The corner of Brad's lips teased, but he kept his eyes on the road, not hinting at more.

"It would be the perfect ending to this day."

"How so?"

"I feel like we've been on a treasure hunt. It was hard not to shop for myself."

"So, I have a design question." He regarded me as we waited at a stoplight. "You're never without a generous portion of glitter or something metallic, and trust me, I'm not saying there's anything wrong with that. I would never want to be the person blamed for dulling your sparkle, as you put it."

"Don't worry. You won't convince me to tone it down again."

"Good, and I shouldn't have asked you to before. But correct me if I'm wrong, nothing you admired or selected today has that same vibe."

"Is there a question?"

"Why so different?" He drove through the intersection into a nondescript shopping center.

"First, we're designing as a team for a client—"

"Yeah, but I watched you gush over antiques and vintage clothes with not a reflective surface in sight."

"I told you I love things with a story, and I can understand that you don't see the connection. I think it's about beauty and wanderlust. Like old stuff is magical, and I like to have a little or a lot of magic in my everyday, so I add a little."

"Some may describe it as a lot." He parked the truck and cut the engine. "But it makes sense to me. Ready for some home cooking?"

My chest filled with an inexplicable amount of emotion, I touched his arm. "Hey, Brad."

"Yeah." As he rested his eyes on mine, a flicker of concern appeared. "Is everything okay?"

"Everything's great. I just wanted to thank you for noticing and asking about all this." I gestured to myself. Besides my normal shimmery eye makeup, the outfit I'd chosen included a large pair of pink glitter teardrop earrings, floral rhinestone-embellished platform sneakers, and a slim metallic pink belt over a simple mint green dress. "It means a lot that you care enough to try to understand me."

"Of course. And you shouldn't worry about making the wrong decisions. You don't always need to check with Wren. You're just as talented. Y'all are just different."

If my heart had been full before, it was absolutely overflowing. How did he get me and know exactly what I needed to hear? I hadn't questioned every selection, but part of that was because we could return anything that didn't work. Still, it was nice that he thought I was talented.

"Thanks," I said, but the lump in my throat prevented me from saying anything else.

"You're welcome. It's not very often that I get to spend an entire day with a fairy." He grinned.

"Just don't expect me to use my magic wand to grant you any wishes." I pinched his arm playfully.

As we strolled to the restaurant, the door swung open. An older couple exited, and Brad stopped moving. "Fantastic," he muttered, almost grumbling.

"Brad, what a pleasant surprise." The woman embraced him.

"Hi, Mom." Brad shifted out of her arms. "Dad." Shaking the man's hand, he did one of those guy-side-hug maneuvers.

"And who do we have here?" With arched brows, Mrs. Chastain looked from me to her son.

"This is Zoe Stockton. She's one of the designers from Chicago, working on the Magnolia Bluff project."

"I see." She gave me a once-over, her gaze halting on my shoes before returning to my face. "Nice to meet you."

"And where's Wren?" Mr. Chastain surveyed the area. "I thought you'd been spending your extra time with her these days."

"Wren's at the house, and this isn't free time. We've been driving all over Pooler, Savannah, Georgetown and some places in between picking up items."

"Sounds like something you should've delegated." His dad frowned.

"We didn't leave until I made sure the subs had their assignments. Wren needed these items, and while it might not have been ideal, this was the best way to get them. She's been in touch all day. Between the two of us, everything is running ahead of schedule."

"And when do we get to meet this wonderful Wren?" Mrs. Chastain asked.

"She'll be at the party. She's looking forward to meeting you too."

Really? I mean, I didn't think Wren was against meeting them, but she certainly hadn't mentioned some desire to befriend Brad's parents. Although I wasn't part of every discussion between them.

"I hope you're taking this job seriously, and I hope this is your last day gallivanting all over the Low Country with Wren's assistant."

Ouch.

"You have no reason to worry," Brad said, and I couldn't help but notice that the guy who'd been complimenting me only moments before didn't correct his dad about my position. But it wasn't like I corrected people when they got it wrong. Assistant might not be my title, but it was my role. Still, I thought Brad saw me as more.

After a stilted goodbye, the Chastains left, and we entered the restaurant. While the food was good, our conversation lagged, and the silence was anything but comfortable. By the time we finished eating, all my previous feelings of bliss had departed, leaving me empty. But at least I knew where I stood with Brad, and I wouldn't hold out hope for anything more. At this point, friendship even felt like a stretch.

Chapter Six

♥

Forty-eight hours later, we weren't only behind schedule, but the muralist had bailed, and Nathaniel had convinced Wren to paint the mural. Any other time, I would've been a ball of mush at the way he championed her, giving her encouragement and attention that he spared no one else.

But with all her time consumed with the painting or him, I was left to lead the rest of the project and organize the party. Not to mention, Brad had apparently decided the friend zone wasn't good enough, so I found myself in the very lonely work-colleague zone, which I didn't even know existed until he arrived at the house on Tuesday.

After a day of his avoiding me, I was glad that I'd scheduled time on Wednesday to work at Nathaniel's house with Bonnie on the final details for the party. At least, I might have a chance of getting a slice of her five-flavor pound cake.

Bonnie stood at the kitchen counter when I entered. "Good morning, honey."

"Is it still morning? It's been a long day already." I plopped onto the banquette in the breakfast nook.

"I have just the thing you need." She removed the glass cover from the top of the cake stand. "Why don't you tell me what's going on while I make us a snack?"

"It's nothing, really."

"Oh, it sounds like something, and from what I've observed, I'm guessing it has more to do with a hunky contractor than the non-appearing muralist."

"Brad and I are just friends. Well, I thought we were anyway."

"Did y'all have a falling out?"

"Not really. Everything was fine until we ran into his parents the other night, and he started acting weird. Wren warned me that Brad was hoping to settle down. For all the obvious reasons, I can't be that woman for him, but why couldn't we at least be friends?"

Bonnie placed a cup of hot tea and a plate with a large piece of cake on the table. "I'm not sure I see obvious reasons." She sat across from me.

"Number one, he's not interested. Number two, I live in Chicago. He lives here. Number three, his parents stared at me like I had two heads and clearly expected Wren. Number four, see number one." I forked a bite of the cake, letting the butter, sugar, and bright lemon flavors temper my frustrations.

"And you'd be happy just being friends?"

"Yes. We get along so well, and to be honest, I need his help. And it's hard to work with someone who's avoiding you and trying to communicate solely through texts."

"Sounds like *he* might not be okay with just being friends." She quirked a brow.

A flutter of hope spun through me, but what about my reasons? Regardless, I was curious what wisdom Bonnie would share, so I asked, "How so?" And then filled my mouth with cake.

"I think it was Shakespeare who wrote that the person who protests too much about something believes the opposite. He's avoiding you because he doesn't trust himself around you. He's attracted to you, honey. I'd bet my top-secret hummingbird cake recipe on it."

"Don't make me prove you wrong, so I can get that recipe."

"I'm not worried. I've been around long enough to know my secret is safe."

I cut another bite. "Maybe, but frankly, I don't have time to concoct a rendezvous with Brad. I simply need him to stay engaged or, better yet, take charge until Wren finishes."

"You may need Brad to do his part, but you're more than capable of this role, so why don't you believe in yourself?" She sipped her tea.

"What if everything falls apart? There are so many decisions to make. What if I choose wrong?" I tapped the tine of my fork on the edge of the plate. "What if the clients hate what I put together, and I take down Wren and Brad with me? He's sure not going to like me then, and he really needs this. So does Wren. This could be a career-defining moment for them."

"And you." She placed her teacup on its saucer. "You can't lead while worrying over what-ifs and doubting yourself, so you have to decide to have confidence in the gifts God's given you and the opportunities. This might feel scary, but you can do it. You've made all the decisions about the party plans."

"But you've helped me." I sipped my tea.

"Not as much as you want to give me credit for, and before Wren arrived, you were running the show. Listen, I get wanting to help your friends be successful, but you don't need to always hide behind them. Sometimes God takes us out of our comfort zone so we can grow. Why don't you see this as a chance to prove to yourself that you can lead this team?"

"I don't really have a choice if I want Wren and Brad to succeed."

"If you have to see it that way to overcome your fear, I guess that's the best we can do."

"Thanks for believing in me and letting me freak out." I pulled out my tablet.

"It's okay to be nervous, but let's channel that energy into something more productive. What do you say?"

"Let's go over the menu and the timing. And after we finish, I'm going to find Brad and make sure we're on the same page as far as the projects go."

"Wonderful. And Zoe, you aren't alone. I'm here, and I think you'll find Brad never left. Maybe he's got stuff going on that you don't know about and needs time to figure out."

"He can have all the time he wants after this party. Until then, I'm going to make sure his energy is focused on the goal." Whatever might have been blooming between us had clearly chosen the wrong season to bud.

"Spoken like a true leader." Bonnie raised her cup for a toast.

I joined her even as my nerves twisted inside me, but I wouldn't let down Wren or Brad.

Armed with a large piece of Bonnie's pound cake, I searched the renovation house for Brad. While I wasn't sure what I'd done to upset him, I figured it couldn't hurt to bring a peace offering. Like Wren was constantly reminding me, we didn't have time for drama. As I passed the kitchen, I breathed a sigh of relief that the counters were finally being installed, and now I had another excuse to talk to Brad. We needed to see if the tile installers could begin early or bring more help to place the backsplash.

The kitchen needed to be completed early so we could use it for the party. While Bonnie could use Nathaniel's kitchen to prepare the food, he still wasn't a fan of the development, and no one, including Wren, wanted to irritate him. We weren't even sure he'd attend the party, but with the way he was doting on Wren, it seemed likely. Still, I didn't want to add appeasing an obstinate, out-spoken neighbor to my list, so I was leaving him up to Wren. With his attitude, I was thankful Bonnie had agreed to help, but she'd made it clear that he didn't control who she worked with.

After checking all the spaces on the first floor for Brad, I climbed the stairs to the second floor. It would not be part of the reveal because the bathrooms wouldn't be completed, but there was still plumbing and electrical work proceeding. The party was only one of our deadlines. We'd given Linda and Fred a move-in date that none of us wanted to extend.

When I entered the bedroom at the back of the house, I found Brad pacing the length of the screened porch with his phone pressed to his ear. I slipped out of the French doors and presented the cake to him. He lifted a finger, letting me know he'd be another minute. He didn't smile, and his normally bright blue eyes seemed muted.

Who'd dulled his sparkle? My muscles tensed defensively. Brad might not have been uber-friendly lately, but he was one of the sweetest guys I'd ever met, a stark contrast from Nathaniel, which made Wren's choice all the stranger. But I didn't want to think about them. I wanted to do whatever it took to get the gleam back in Brad's eyes.

"Just keep me in the loop. Thanks." Brad ended the call. "Is something wrong?"

"Not that I know of, but I was going to ask you the same thing."

"I was trying to see if we could get a head start on the backsplash, since the counters are going to be in early. They couldn't give me a definitive answer." He pointed at my face. "You sure nothing's wrong? When you walked out here, you looked kind of, I don't know, mad or worried."

"It's nothing." I smiled widely, batting my lashes. "Better?"

He cringed. "Not exactly." But then his lips twitched up, and he chuckled. It was quite possibly the best thing I'd heard in days, and that morning I'd been awoken by a songbird outside my window. It reminded me of summer campouts in the backyard. I hadn't heard a bird early in the morning in years. It was too noisy in the city.

Feeling like I'd at least accomplished one thing today, I relaxed my expression into something less laughable and held up the cake. "Bonnie sent this over for you."

Brad took the plate. "How are the party plans going? Do you need any help? I could call my mom?"

"Tempting, but we have it under control." And even if we didn't, his mom wouldn't be who I'd ask for help.

"Great. Did you need something else?"

"Actually, I was going to see if we could get the backsplash installed early, but great minds." I pointed between us. "And on that note, I wanted to let you know I plan to do everything I can to make this reveal party a success."

"I never doubted you." He peered into my eyes with an intensity that sent electricity all the way to my toes, but even in the moment, I held my breath, waiting for the *but*. And counting because Virginia's method for calming me had become almost second nature when I was stressed. And while I didn't think this sensation was stress, adrenaline was definitely zipping through my veins.

When he said nothing else, and I realized I might pass out from lack of oxygen because I'd counted way past three, I exhaled. "Thanks."

"You sure you're okay?" His brows drew together as he studied me.

"Yes, of course."

"Wait, where's your glittery makeup? I knew something wasn't right."

Really? He'd noticed? I touched my eyelid. "With everything going on, I didn't feel like it."

"But what about the magic?" Brad dropped his focus.

"I didn't think you cared."

"Maybe you don't realize how much you care about something until it's gone." He returned his attention to me. He seemed to be talking about more than makeup.

"I get that." I fought to maintain a nonchalant expression as mini-fireworks exploded under my skin,. "If I didn't say it the other day, thanks for pitching in and showing me around. Dinner was delicious."

"You're welcome, but I'm pretty sure you thanked me, and I probably should confess that it didn't feel like work." He grinned.

"Well, that's a relief." I wiped my brow dramatically. "I had way too much fun to call it work, but you know that saying, find a way to make money doing what you love, and you'll never work a day in your life."

"Yeah, that may be true, but don't tell my dad." His expression clouded, and now I was certain who was tarnishing Brad's joy.

"It may not be a consolation, but I think you're doing a great job, and so do Wren and our clients. Your parents are going to be so proud of you."

"We'll see. Actually, I should thank you for letting me be totally real with you. I'm sorry I got a little moody after we saw my parents, and I appreciate you not holding it against me. They can be judgy, and I let my guard down with you. It was just whiplash running into them, and a reminder that I have to take this job seriously."

"But it's okay to have fun too."

"Not when it comes to me and work. At least that's my dad's opinion."

"Okay." I clasped my hands under my chin. "Well, it's a good thing he's not here and has given you the chance with this project. So how about we agree that we're going to work hard together, and if we feel like eating cake and laughing now and then, it'll be our secret."

"You're the best boss."

"Literally, no one has ever called me their boss, and I have two younger siblings, so that's saying something. I just hope I don't let everyone down."

"We got this, boss." He slung an arm around my shoulders. "Ready to eat cake and check the punch list?"

"I already had cake, but I'm happy to work while you indulge."

"This day keeps getting better." He squeezed me to his side, filling me with warmth and hope.

Chapter Seven

♥

I'd never imagined that facing my fears could be so much fun and so freeing. Since college, I'd always been too scared to take the chance. It didn't hurt that Brad had my back, and Bonnie sent daily texts of encouragement. Still, I was the one deciding about key design elements and for the presentation we'd give at the party. People were reporting to me, and I was leading them.

Sure, my palms sweated—a lot—but I wiped off my hands and the worry, and we moved on with the project. I'd needed to be pushed out of my comfort zone like Bonnie said, but now that I had taken the step, I was loving it. Cautiously loving it, but loving it nonetheless.

It wasn't just the work. I was growing fond of the location and the people, especially one person, but I was keeping those feelings under control. Okay, not really. I expected my heart and stomach to take turns flipping when his blue eyes caught mine and when his smile crinkled the edges of them. But that had nothing on when he stood close, and I was enveloped in his scent, like a patchwork quilt of comfort. But the worst was when he touched me, either by accident or in a friendly hug. Heck, my knees had nearly given out when he'd high-fived me after the inspector nodded his approval during our tour today.

I leaned against the door frame, watching Brad escort him to his car. When he turned around, he was beaming. My heart hammered like it wanted to escape my body and meet Brad halfway. Thankfully, my legs and feet behaved and listened obediently to my brain.

"He said we're all good and will have his report complete by Monday!" Brad wrapped his arms around me and lifted me off the ground, swinging me in a circle.

I gasped. This kind of hug was extra even for Brad, but after the initial shock, I gripped him just as tight and absorbed everything I couldn't name but felt to my core.

"Sorry. Too much?" He slowly lowered me to the ground, but he didn't move away.

"No—" I held onto his arms, staring at his chest. "It's fantastic news." But my words came out all breathy because my lungs had decided that inhaling oxygen wasn't necessary.

"You sure?"

I swallowed, refusing to shift my gaze to his. "Yep."

I needed to let go of him, but he was holding me too. We needed space because the energy crackling between us might cause a spontaneous combustion and definitely rocket us out of the friend zone.

Brad shifted slightly, moving one hand to my arm. "Good because the last week, working side by side with you every day has kind of been amazing." His thumb traced a lazy circle on my wrist, sending thrills skating over my skin. "And even though I want this project to stay on schedule and be completed on time, I sort of want to delay it because finishing it means you'll be leaving."

"Really?" I focused on his thumb until it stopped moving.

"Zoe, please look at me. I can't tell what you're thinking, and I don't want to make things awkward if you haven't been feeling this thing between us."

"I'm feeling it too." As I met his gaze, I tucked my lip between my teeth. Why was this so hard? This friendship had seemed like a good idea, but it just made everything between us mean more.

"Hey." The lines of concern between his eyes faded as his attention fell to my lips for a moment. "So still awkward but better?"

"Better. I wasn't sure if it was just me, especially with all the Wren stuff, and also, I want to respect your focus on the job. I didn't—don't—want to be a distraction."

The corners of his lips twitched with amusement.

"What?"

"Nothing." He smirked, and while it might be seen as a negative on any other face, it was still beautiful on Brad.

"No, I want to know." I pulled back. "I don't think anything I said was funny."

"Hold on." He clasped my arms, holding me close, but he'd let me go if I tried to escape.

I definitely wouldn't. Mostly because I was pretty certain that if I left his hold, my legs would fail me. "I'm listening."

"I'll tell you what I was thinking, but you have to promise not to get mad."

"Fine. I promise." But I provided him with a playful pout, countering his irritatingly adorable smirk.

"It's just that you often reflect more light than a disco ball, so it's hard to believe you don't think you're slightly distracting."

"Point taken, but you know that's not what I meant."

"I do, but it doesn't mean that you being in the same space with me doesn't grab my attention. Trust me, I've tried to ignore you and pretend I could keep you in the friend zone, but it's not working."

"In some ways that's a relief to hear, but in other ways, it complicates matters. There are very valid reasons we shouldn't take our relationship to the next level." As my words hit my ears, I kind of wanted to pat myself on the back for how mature they sounded, but also smack my forehead because I did want to kiss him. I had wanted to kiss him for days, and now he might not.

"So—" With enviable skill, he slid one hand from my arm to my back and moved the other to cup my face. "You don't want to do this?" Then his thumb was brushing over my bottom lip, and I was quivering.

Was I hot? Was I cold? Did it matter?

"I didn't say that," I whispered, really glad he didn't seem interested in logistics.

"Oh, sorry." Wren said, her voice throwing us apart like she'd shoved us. "I noticed the inspector left and was hoping we were going to celebrate with those cupcakes you made. I'm starving, and—" She winced and gave a quick wave as she backed away. "On second thought, I'll leave you alone." She turned and darted around the corner.

"Wren, it's fine. Just give us a minute." Trying unsuccessfully not to giggle, I collapsed against Brad, burying my face in his chest.

"I'm not finding this as funny as you," he said, but I could hear the tease in his voice as his fingers linked with mine.

I blew out the last of my laughter as I turned my head to the side. "Sorry, but our timing seriously stinks."

"In more ways than one." Chuckling, he dropped a kiss on the top of my head.

With the mood completely ruined, I shifted away from him. "At least we can laugh about it."

"I'd rather the alternative."

"We should probably go." I tugged him toward the door. "Look at the bright side; you get a celebratory cupcake."

"Poor substitute, but it'll do." He stopped and spun me to face him, peering into my eyes. "For now."

For now!

With my insides melting, I somehow managed to turn around and walk through the door, but those words would play on repeat until *later* arrived.

After two days, I was almost certain Brad and I wouldn't have to worry about continuing what we'd started until after the reveal party because we were rarely alone for more than a moment. I'd thought Wren would ask me about what she'd seen, but after we ate our cupcakes, she'd gone to Nathaniel's house. And with Fred and Linda expecting a tour when they arrived, my relationship with Brad wasn't a topic of conversation, especially with painting the mural taking up most of her time. And I was glad for the time to process and find my center.

But while I didn't want to discuss the almost-kiss with Wren, I definitely wanted to explore the topic with Brad. Unfortunately, work was all-consuming, so I'd resigned myself that it was for the best. At least that is what I told myself, but Brad was no help, sending me sweet texts, grazing the back of his hand against mine when we passed, and letting his attention linger on me during meetings.

By Wednesday night, my nerves hummed with energy that needed an outlet. After I'd baked a batch of lemon squares that I planned to give to Linda and Fred when they arrived the next day, I got my phone to cue up a playlist for a personal dance party. Instead, it chimed with an incoming text.

> Brad: Are you available for a quick chat?

> Me: Yes, is something wrong?

> Brad: No, I just need your directions. Can you meet me at the house?

> Me: Sure. OTW.

I'd thought he'd said he wasn't coming back when he left before lunch. As I exited the cottage, I tried to ignore the worry niggling inside me.

Instead, I practiced my breathing exercises. Across the river, the sun silhouetted the tall trees in front of a brilliant pink sky. Even if the designs weren't perfect, the natural beauty of the bluff would sell this location.

I entered the dimly lit great room. "Wren? Brad?"

"She's gone for the night." Brad appeared across the room.

Gasping, I clutched my chest. "You spooked me."

"I'm sorry." He crossed the room and took my hand.

"It's fine. What's up? Is there a reason all the lights are off? Oh, no, please tell me there isn't an electrical problem."

"Relax." He squeezed my hand. "There's not an electrical problem. I just didn't want to draw attention and get interrupted."

"Ooo-kay." My pulse raced.

"Are you sure?"

"Yes, of course."

"Good." He reached into his back pocket and retrieved a bandana. "I have a surprise, and you seem like the type to peek." He moved behind me. "Is this okay? I'm not freaking you out?"

"I'm absolutely freaking out but in all the good ways. Hurry up and tie that thing on." Bouncing on my toes, I shut my eyes. "But you were wrong. I'd never peek. I love surprises." And the way Brad continued to show me different parts of himself. He could be so serious around everyone else, but when it was just us, he let his playful side out.

Chuckling, he settled a hand on my shoulder. "Okay, but you have to be still."

"Right. When did you get back?" I held the front of the material over my eyes while he secured it.

"A while ago, but I waited until Wren finished for the day before I texted you." He led me through the house.

"So this is a secret, surprise rendezvous?"

"If that makes it better, then yes, but manage your expectations. I'm a pretty regular guy."

"You're so much more than you give yourself credit for. You're generous, smart, charming—"

"Zoe, stop—" And before I could protest, he scooped me up, cradling me against his chest. "I wasn't angling for compliments, but thank you. I'm glad you have such a high opinion of me. Hopefully, it's not too high."

Even if I'd wanted to tell him that nothing could top being swept off my feet and carried to a surprise, I no longer had the lung capacity to breathe deeply, much less utter another word. One day I'd explain to Brad that taking a girl's breath away always results in elevating a guy way beyond regular. I mean, this was the stuff of fairytales, and sorry, but any girl who claims to be offended hasn't been carried out of the tower by her hero. It's seriously heady stuff.

I happily snuggled a little closer into Brad's muscled chest and tried to wait patiently for what I hoped would finally be a kiss. His shoes echoed on the wood floors of what I surmised was the staircase, and as we reached the top, the scent of something delicious wafted around us.

"Zoe, you're very quiet. Did I do something wrong? Was this too much? I probably sounded like an oaf."

I giggled. "That's what Nathaniel calls you."

"I'm glad you don't let his opinion sway you."

"Never, and I'm fine, better than fine."

"I'm glad you're good." He lowered my feet to the ground and removed the blindfold.

I smiled up at him. "I'm great."

Grinning, he turned me around. "Surprise."

In the center of the empty room was a bistro table with an electric lantern in the center, giving off just enough light to make the scene romantic and not eerie. Outside, the new landscape lights shone on the limbs of the live oak and magnolia trees, creating a magical canopy of branches and leaves.

"Oh, wow. This is beautiful." Covering my mouth, I crossed the room. "I can't believe you did all this."

"I've been wanting to do something special since we got interrupted."

"Well, this is definitely special." I spun around and embraced him, tilting my face. "But you didn't need to do all this. I've been ready to pick up where we left off."

Brad stared back at me for a moment before he shook his head. "Good to know, and we'll get to all that, but first—" Brad disengaged my arms, turned me around, and pulled out a chair—"I have a gift for you." He presented a wrapped box. "I hope you like it."

"Thank you." I removed the paper.

"It's an antique recipe box like my nana's. I saw it when we were shopping."

"I love it."

He sat, draping an arm around my shoulders. "Open it."

"There's more? You're spoiling me." As warmth gathered in my stomach, I removed the top of the box and withdrew two cards. A recipe was printed on each of them.

"Those are Nana's hummingbird cake and pecan pie recipes."

"For real?" I tried to read them in the dim light.

"Absolutely."

"This is honestly one of the most thoughtful gifts anyone has ever given me. I take it all back. I'm definitely glad you put this all together. Thank you so much." When I shifted to give him my full attention, he gazed back.

I dropped the cards and inhaled a shaky breath as Brad drew us closer together.

"You're welcome." With a touch that seemed almost too soft for his size and strength, he cradled my face, sweeping his thumb along my cheekbone, sending shivers through my body.

As my eyes feathered closed, Brad's lips met mine, gently and with careful consideration. He guided me through the kiss, and I followed like we were dancing across an empty ballroom with a string quartet playing just for us. After so much waiting, the release of energy left me floating blissfully, my body humming with each caress of Brad's mouth. I certainly hadn't needed to manage my expectations because this kiss with Brad far exceeded anything I'd ever experienced or known to hope for.

When our lips finally parted, Brad continued to hold me close, tracing the back of my arm. Out of breath and brimming with emotions, we didn't say anything, just relished in the moment.

Brad pecked my cheeks and then my forehead playfully and then straightened. "I did bring dessert if you want it." He twirled a lock of my hair.

While I adored his thoughtfulness, it was this light-hearted way he behaved when it was just the two of us that turned my insides to mush. And with a quick move, I caught his face, giggling as I pressed my lips to his. "Dessert can wait," I said between kisses.

"Yes, ma'am." His laugh tickled my lips.

Who knew kissing and laughing was a thing? And as the night continued, I decided it would become one of my favorite things.

Chapter Eight

♥

There's nothing quite like sugar and kisses for happy dreams. The next morning as I crossed the yard to meet Brad for a final walk-through before Linda and Fred arrived, I refrained from humming a cheerful tune but not from a few skips and one spin. And when I twirled through the back door and into Brad's arms, I relished in the bubbles of bliss bursting inside me.

"Good morning, sunshine." Brad pressed a kiss to my lips that I'm sure he meant to be quick, but neither of us retreated, instead lingering in our newly discovered hobby. But after far too short a time, Brad pulled back. He took what I'm sure he thought was an artful assessment of the area, but when his eyes landed back on me, his brows tugged together. "We probably shouldn't do too much of that while we're supposed to be working."

"How much would you consider too much?"

He frowned slightly, moving out of reach. "We should probably set some boundaries."

"Fine." With all the dramatics of a teenage girl, I dropped my shoulders and sighed. We'd barely started having fun. Did we really need to have a define the relationship talk now?

"I think we should keep things on the down low. The clients are coming today, and the party is this weekend. We've both got a lot riding on this."

"Sure. I get it. Obviously, we'll be professional. I would never do anything to mess this up for you."

"Good. I'm glad we're on the same page." He raked his fingers through his hair, and somehow it looked even better, but his face was still lined with tension. "I just can't start something serious right now. I don't want you to think I'm not into you because I am, but I need to be focused."

"Relax. I'm not one of those girls who organizes a wedding after one date and a few kisses, no matter how fantastic they were. Besides, I don't even know my plans beyond completing this project." Although I'd begun feeling like I wanted to stay in Georgia and work on this more confident version of myself without all the trappings of my life in Chicago. Here, I was forced to stand on my own, be decisive, and own my choices. At first, it'd been scary, but as I'd worked with Bonnie and Brad, I'd realized a strength I didn't know I had, and I liked it.

"Ooo-kay?" He drew out the word like he was questioning his agreement, and he probably was. He was such a good guy and likely concerned about my feelings, so I needed to put him at ease. I certainly didn't want to end our relationship before it'd even begun. We'd been taking it slow for weeks, and the results had been far from disappointing. In my expert opinion, delayed gratification definitely had its perks.

"How about if we make a deal? For now, when it's appropriate, we'll have fun, live in the moment, but when it's work time, we'll just be co-workers." I extended my hand, waiting for him to shake on it.

"I can agree to that." As he grasped my hand, he quickly surveyed the space, and then pulled me close to his body. With his lips a breath away from mine, he stopped and grinned. "But we should definitely kiss on it."

"What was I think—" Before I could finish, Brad's mouth was over mine, sealing our deal, and making sure I didn't forget that while he might have a serious side, he was his most real self with me.

Shivers of desire and fear collided in my chest. I might have talked a good game of indifference, but whatever was happening with Brad wasn't like anything I'd experienced before.

With a final press of his lips to mine, Brad released me, leaving both of us slightly breathless. "Sorry."

"Don't be. You were right."

He smirked. "It's probably not the best idea, but for now, I don't want to *think* or *talk* anymore about what we're doing." He gently pulled down a ringlet next to my face and then let it go.

"Thinking is overrated anyway."

"Thanks for being so amazing and understanding and everything I need right now. Our time together is the only time I feel like I can relax and be myself."

"Glad to help, and don't give me too much credit. I'm enjoying my part of the bargain." I bounced my brows, but truthfully, he was making me a better person too. He was a huge part of my growth as a leader. I'd always seen Wren as my superior, even if she didn't. But with Brad, we relied on each other's strengths to help the other in an equal partnership. Not that I would tell him and freak him out more. Besides it'd probably freak me out just as much to say it out loud.

"We should get to work." Brad checked his watch. "Linda and Fred will be here soon."

"Right." I lowered my hand in front of my face, like I'd seen actors do when getting into character. "Where should we start?"

"Master bath." Brad pressed his lips into a thin line, but the corner twitched just enough to let me know his playful side was barely below the surface, and I couldn't wait until the next time we met.

Just the thought blasted an electrical charge out from my middle to every part of my body, leaving me buzzing with anticipation.

While it might've been good to have some time and space to understand what I was feeling, I didn't believe kissing Brad would be a problem for my heart, and Brad managed his emotions expertly.

Did that mean he wasn't as invested in us as much as me?

Nope. I would not think any more about our future. I'd promised to live in the moment, and that's what I'd do. My heart would be fine.

Even I realized sequins are supposed to be reserved for evening attire. Not that I don't sneak a dusting in every so often on one of my daytime outfits. So given the chance to shimmer in a party dress at the reveal, you'd better believe I'd be covered in sequins. Fuchsia sequins to be exact. The color reminded me of the azaleas blossoming around the bluff.

With puffed sleeves, a fitted bodice, and a tiered skirt that fluttered above my knees, it'd be the perfect dress for the reveal party. The two oversized satin bows that secured the back made the dress interesting from all angles. Not wanting to overdo it, I'd used my favorite gold and pale green glittery eye shadow and misted my hair with glitter spray. I kept my accessories and shoes simple, even though I had a beaded floral headband that would have been amazing. The house was supposed to be the star of the show, and I didn't want to be a distraction.

Although if Brad did a double take, I'd be okay with that. We'd only managed to catch a few very brief moments alone over the last couple of days, so tonight I had a plan to meet him before the party. I'd told him I wanted to go over our talking points, so we made a good impression on the guests, but I certainly hadn't invited Wren to our rehearsal.

After gliding on a final coat of glossy lipstick the same shade as my dress, I checked my appearance in the mirror. I'd definitely achieved the right balance of sparkle and shine. I'd have to find somewhere else to wear this dress where I could amp up my accessories and makeup. Surely, there was a club in Savannah.

As I walked to the door—okay, I may have danced a little, but who could resist a shimmy when wearing this ensemble?—I heard a knock. Wren had gone over to the house earlier, and Brad was supposed to meet me in the study. Hopefully, it wouldn't be Nathaniel. He was fine in small doses, and with Wren, he was almost charming, but he was not happy about this party, and I didn't want him to cast a shadow over my bright mood.

Without a real choice, I opened the door, and I'm glad I did.

Smiling his most charming smile that lit up his entire face, especially his blue eyes, was Brad, wearing a dark suit and holding a bouquet of lilies and tulips. "Since we can't go on an actual date right now, and after we enter the house, we will need to be professional, I wanted to have a few minutes alone."

"Me too." *Wow*! I didn't think it was possible, but Brad was even more attractive in a suit. All kinds of fireworks were exploding inside me, and I wanted to smother him in kisses, but I needed to stay calm, or I'd wreck my appearance. Instead, I settled for inhaling his spicy scent of cinnamon and cedar and shifted out of his way. "That's why I planned the meeting."

"I figured, but it didn't seem private enough." As he entered, he gave me the flowers and pecked my cheek.

"Thank you. They're beautiful." I carried the bouquet to the kitchen area. The guest cottage was last on the reno list, so the décor was in one word, sad. "These will brighten up the space." I placed the flowers in a glass pitcher, filled it with water, and put them in the center of the small table.

Brad laced his fingers with mine. "Lilies and tulips because I think you said they're your favorites."

"You're right." I pressed my palm over my heart as it filled with too much emotion. First, the antique recipe box with his Nana's recipes and now these flowers. Sure, I'd had guys bring me flowers and even give me a few gifts, but none of them had ever taken the time to listen to me and present me with things that meant more because of what they represented. Maybe he was always this thoughtful with his gifts. Actually, I was almost certain that he wouldn't give something to someone without it holding a special meaning. As my entire body radiated with warmth, any plans to keep my heart out of our relationship ended. And honestly, I didn't care. I wanted more of these feelings and more of Brad.

"I'm glad." He twirled one of my ringlets. "By the way, before we get caught up in whatever awaits us, I need to tell you how beautiful you are and how amazing everything you've organized and executed will be tonight." He released the curl and slid his fingers to my back.

"Thank you." I focused my gaze on his. Normally, I'd have launched into a speech about how it'd been a team effort, but he knew that. Besides, I could barely breathe in his arms, much less talk.

"I don't want to mess you up."

But I didn't care anymore. Clasping the back of his head, I rose on my toes and pressed my lips to his, and Brad didn't hold back either as he responded with intense concentration. I didn't want the moment to end. I wanted time to stop. Melting under his touch, I yielded the last of my resolve to him. Whatever happened tonight would always be insignificant compared to this time we'd shared, and no matter what, I'd always hold it dear.

But my bliss was unfortunately interrupted by the buzzing of Brad's phone, and his abrupt reaction as he nearly leaped away from me, snatching his phone from his pocket. Personally, I'd have ignored the noise and the message. But the way the color drained from his face as he regarded his screen, stopped me from voicing my displeasure. Even the dusting of glitter on his cheeks and jacket couldn't bring light to his expression or the pit forming in my stomach.

"Is everything okay?" I crept closer to him.

"Yeah. It's just I didn't mean for this to happen." Frowning, he pointed between us, and I wasn't sure if he meant our most recent rendezvous or our relationship. He tucked his phone back into his pocket. "My parents are almost here. We need to get over to the house. Linda asked me to invite you for a toast before the guests arrived. She said it with a wink, so I think she believes something's going on between us. I ignored her, but be aware that we need to be on our guard tonight. I don't want anyone getting the wrong idea."

Even though I knew his parents had a chilling effect on him, his words hit me like a round of punches to the gut. "Then I guess we better get a move on. I'm sorry I distracted you." I strode for the door.

But Brad got there before me, curse those long legs, and held it open. "Zoe, please know that whatever happens tonight, I do care for you. Our timing just stinks."

"Fine." I proceeded without a glance in his direction. If I was going to pretend there was nothing between us, I needed to gather my composure on the very brief walk.

Apparently lost in his own thoughts, Brad said nothing as we made our way into the house. Linda and Fred waved us over to a table with five flutes of champagne as Wren crossed the space from the front door. "The shuttle with our guests is pulling into the drive."

"Everyone, grab a glass." Linda raised hers and passed one to Fred as the rest of us chose our own. "Thank you for everything you've done. The renovations are a glorious success, and we know the clubhouse will be even better. Congratulations!"

As we clinked flutes, a server holding a tray of drinks opened the front door for the potential clients. After a small sip of my champagne, I returned it to a tray. With my emotional state already faltering, the last thing I needed was alcohol. My most immediate concern was putting some distance between Brad and me.

But before I could move, he leaned close to my ear and whispered, "They're here. I'm sorry."

Even as his warm breath alerted my senses, my gut clenched when his words registered. *I'm sorry*. What?

But I didn't have time to ask for clarification before he said, "Mom, Dad, y'all remember Zoe. She works with Wren."

"Oh, right." Mr. Chastain nodded.

While Mrs. Chastain took me in, she gave me a tight smile. "Aren't you adorable? Fairy-like with all that sparkle."

"It seemed like the right occasion to be festive." I smiled widely, refusing to give her the pleasure of knowing her insincere compliment had hit.

"That's a thought," she said, turning her attention to her son. "Brad, everything looks wonderful."

"Yes, son. It's good to see you've finally taken something seriously and worked hard to make it a success."

"Yes, our Brad managed for a long time on his charm." Mrs. Chastain patted Brad on the cheek. "It's amazing how you can have two children who are complete opposites. Carleigh was always so responsible and a go-getter, but over the years, we learned to expect something different from you. Now, you're proving us wrong."

No longer able to contain myself, I said, "Brad has been integral to the success of this project. He's proactive and diligent. You should be proud of him."

"Of course, we are, and it's nice that he has someone to cheer him on." Brad's mother smiled, but I could see the displeasure in her eyes. "Y'all seem to be spending a lot of time together." She arched a brow and then brushed what was left of the glitter from Brad's jacket. It wasn't much, but it was enough to turn Brad's cheeks red.

"It's all work." Brad gestured toward the owner's suite. "Why don't I give y'all a quick tour? I'm sure Zoe needs to greet the other guests."

"Right. Have fun." I hurried to the safety of the kitchen and Bonnie's level head. I needed someone to tell me that I wasn't going crazy.

Chapter Nine

♥

Apparently, I do my best work when I'm slightly off kilter. I never made it to the kitchen. Instead, Linda had stopped me and introduced me to Walter Tolleson and his wife, *the* Cheryl Tolleson, executive for the Living Well Network.

Calling on the poise and grace I'd learned as a young dancer, I'd greeted the woman who could change all our lives. Once the introductions were complete, Linda asked me to escort the Tollesons to the dining room where Fred was waiting to show them the mural. Then she'd hurried off, saying that she was going to find Wren and Brad so they could also meet Cheryl.

In the dining room, Fred entertained the Tollesons, giving them the sales pitch for the Retreat at Magnolia Bluff. From what I gleaned between my own swirling thoughts, Fred was good at his job, and with the Tollesons occupied, I slipped away and made another attempt at getting to the safety of the kitchen and my therapy session with Bonnie. I needed someone to assure me that Brad hadn't been a figment of my imagination.

His parents might be condescending and tactless, but how could I excuse the way he'd treated me? Maybe I'd misjudged him. But I still wanted to give him a chance to explain. For a chance outside of this odd set of circumstances where nothing seemed real, but the consequences were huge.

I paused in the butler's pantry that connected the dining room with the kitchen and waited for Bonnie to return.

One thing was clear from the conversation with his parents—Brad needed this win, and until I was sure he'd gotten it, I'd stand by his side. That being said, we didn't need Mr. Chastain to give Cheryl Tolleson his opinion of her home improvement shows.

I needed to run interference, and while I had zero desire to enter another conversation with the Chastains, it seemed like the best way to manage the situation and hopefully help improve their opinion of Brad at the same time.

But first, I inhaled slowly and deeply, counted to five, and exhaled. Although the oxygen to my brain helped, I was still jittery, and I would be until we'd successfully navigated this night. Unfortunately, I needed to exit the butler's pantry to make that happen, and I didn't have time for a chat with Bonnie.

Zoe, you can do this!

With renewed determination, I strode into the kitchen and ran smack into Nathaniel. "Sorry."

"No worries." He steadied me. "Is everything okay?"

"Yep. I just need to find Brad's parents." I backed toward the great room.

"Okay. Have you seen Wren?"

"Check the dining room. Linda wanted her to meet one of the guests in there."

He lifted a half-eaten barbecue slider. "Thanks. I'll head that way in a minute."

"Fantastic." I dashed away, hoping I didn't appear rude. Nathaniel was growing less prickly with every encounter, and I didn't want to set us back to where we'd started. However, it was not at the top of my list of priorities at the moment.

At the edge of the great room, I stopped and did a quick survey. The Chastains were strolling inside from the porch, and if I had to throw my body on the floor like I'd fainted to stop them from progressing to the dining room, that's what I'd do. Thankfully, I didn't need to employ such dramatics because they stopped at a table.

When I approached them, they smiled politely, if a little coldly, but I took my wins where I could. "I thought you might need a new tour guide. Linda mentioned she was going to steal Brad away to introduce him to some of the guests." I gestured to the side of the house opposite the dining room. "Brad is so modest. He probably didn't tell you that Linda and Fred are planning to recommend Chastain Construction to new buyers."

Mr. Chastain rapped his knuckles on the table. "The business would be nice." If he knew anything about current trends, he'd be encouraging the TV show deal with Cheryl Tolleson. It would make their company the most sought-after in the area. Hopefully, we could convince him later.

"Zoe, I'd really like to meet Wren? I'm so pleased she could use my suggestions for so much of the furnishings. I see several pieces I recognize. Do you know where she is?" Mrs. Chastain scanned the room.

"We can keep an eye out for her while we tour the rest of the house. Have you seen the study?"

"I'm sure you're very knowledgeable, but frankly, honey, we'd prefer if Wren or Brad could show us around." Well, at least she was being honest, and if I hadn't known better, I might not have caught the dig. But I learned in my short time in the south that the thicker and sweeter the accent, the more likely you were being insulted, and Mrs. Chastain's words almost sounded melodic.

Unfortunately, the only solution seemed to be finding Wren, and I was running out of ideas until I spotted Bonnie carrying a small tray of desserts. "Have you met Bonnie?" I waved her over. "She prepared all of this amazing food."

"Y'all must be Brad's parents." Bonnie placed the tray on the table. "You must be so proud of him."

"We are, and your food is delicious." Mrs. Chastain chose a lemon square. "Do you do much catering?"

"Bonnie, tell them about your preserves and jellies. I'll go find Wren and Brad." I arched my brows at Bonnie as I finished.

Hoping she'd occupy Brad's parents for a while, I made a beeline for the dining room to get Wren and bring her to the Chastains, but also keep them as far from Cheryl Tolleson as possible. It'd be fine.

With my mind spinning, I hurried into the room. But my feet stopped at the entry, I had to be seeing things. Brad had his arm wrapped around Wren's shoulders like they were a couple, and time seemed to slow as I tried to register what I was witnessing.

"There you are," I heard myself say, everything in me falling as I stared, letting my lips drop into a frown. Of course, she was here. It's why I'd come. As I sensed everyone's eyes focusing on me, I saw Cheryl Tolleson. Thankfully my brain remembered the real goal of my mission. I wouldn't let Brad ruin this opportunity for Wren or him.

After a quick shake of my head to clear my thoughts, I snapped my lips into a smile. "Your parents were looking for you and wanted to meet Wren."

"Brad's father owns the construction company." Wren offered a bowl of cheese straws as she slipped away from Brad. "Zoe and Bonnie have created a tasty sampling of southern foods. You must try one of these cheesy treats." Wren shifted closer to Cheryl and further away from Brad like she didn't want to be under his arm, and of course, she didn't.

Nathaniel would ruin everything if he saw them together. Even if she wasn't admitting it, she'd fallen hard for the author.

Cheryl chose one of the wafers. "And who is Bonnie? Is she also on your team?"

Wren chuckled. "I wish, but I don't think her current employer would be too happy if we stole her away."

"Bonnie is Nathaniel Sullivan's housekeeper," Linda said.

"Ah, yes, the author with the house next door." Cheryl sipped from her glass.

Linda gestured out of the room. "He's here."

"He actually was headed this way, but I guess he got sidetracked." I checked over my shoulder, relieved he wasn't witnessing this scene and kicking myself for telling him where to find Wren.

"Would you like to meet him?" Linda asked Cheryl.

"At some point, but what I'd really like is a tour of the rest of this house and to see the designs and samples for the clubhouse." She pointed her glass at Brad, Wren, and me. "I'm always on the lookout for new talent, and you guys might have that rare and magical thing that makes for fantastic television."

"I told you that you'd be impressed with them." Linda proceeded to the hall.

"It was nice to meet you all. We'll be in touch." Cheryl followed Linda from the room.

Refusing to let Brad ruin this moment and relieved that Cheryl was less likely to meet the Chastains, I grabbed Wren's hands. "I can't believe this is happening. Cheryl thinks we make magic."

While I bounced on my toes, Wren just nodded in a sort of daze. At least I wasn't the only one feeling overwhelmed.

"What's all the excitement?" Mr. Chastain asked from the edge of the room. Bonnie had held them off just long enough, and I couldn't help but feel a little extra cause for celebration.

Mrs. Chastain glanced at her husband. "It must be good news, honey."

Brad winced, his lips pursing as he strode across the room. "It's great news." But his voice was stern as he clasped my shoulder, anchoring me to the floor. "You've met Zoe." Then he took Wren's hand and guided her to his parents. "This is the lead designer, Wren Frazier."

"But Zoe and I work more as a team on our projects or like co-captains." Wren greeted Brad's parents. "It's so nice to meet you, Mr. and Mrs. Chastain. You must be so proud of Brad's work. He has been invaluable to our success and—"

With crazy bad timing, Nathaniel chose that moment to step around the corner. Once his gaze landed on Brad's hand wrapped around Wren's, she stopped talking. I'm not even sure she was breathing.

Nathaniel glared, his eyes darkening. "I wanted to let you know I'm leaving," he said before he pivoted and exited through the front door. He might not have slammed the door, instead calmly shutting it, but the air in the room still seemed to be sucked out with him.

Oblivious to the awkward moment, Mrs. Chastain reached in her oversized designer bag and presented a copy of *A Gardenia Promise.* "Well, that's unfortunate. I'd hoped to convince him to sign my book, but you did say he could be temperamental. I guess that's part of the whole artist persona." She frowned as she dropped the book into the bag.

With worry etched on her forehead, Wren held out her hand to Mrs. Chastain. "I might can catch him if you want me to get your book signed. Mr. Sullivan only took a short break from his newest project to join us tonight. I'm sure he was struck by inspiration and needed to return home." Wren beckoned with her fingers. "But I need to hurry."

"Thank you. I love his stories." Mrs. Chastain shoved the book at Wren. "You are such a wonderful girl, just like Brad described, but even prettier in person."

As Wren hurried from the house, I took my cue to find some peace in the kitchen. Unfortunately, Bonnie was too busy to talk, but I still hid in the breakfast nook with a glass of iced tea, hoping no one else needed me. I'm not sure why I thought it would work, especially with Wren abandoning the party. But thankfully, I had enough time to recharge before Linda and Brad found me.

"We need you to help Brad present the plans for the clubhouse." Linda seized my glass and placed it on the table.

"Happy to help." I shot Brad a side-eye as I stood. "Sure you don't want Wren, the lead designer, to help?"

"She's not back from Nathaniel's. Besides you know as much if not more about the locally sourced items." He reached for me.

But I crossed my arms over my chest. "I'm glad you noticed. Let's do this." And we did. I'm still not sure how, but everything went smoothly and so naturally. As we talked to the group, I forgot to be mad at Brad and enjoyed our give and take, finishing each other's sentences, making little jokes, complimenting each other's gifts and talents. From the smiles on the guests' faces, especially Cheryl's, it seemed like we'd shined. And really, what more could you want?

Chapter Ten

One of the most important things girls learned in college is the therapeutic properties of ice cream, and thankfully, Wren knew that there was peach ice cream that Bonnie had left in the freezer. When she brought it, along with pound cake, to the guest cottage for our pity party, I actually thought everything might be okay.

Everything would be fine, even if things didn't work out with Brad long term. They rarely did anyway. I shouldn't have let myself hope for a different result this time.

Wren wrenched the lid off the ice cream container. "What a night." She held up the ice cream scoop for emphasis.

After we'd finished the presentation, Wren told me that Brad's parents had left when she'd returned with the signed book, which only reminded me of Brad's rude behavior. There might be an explanation, but I wasn't in the mood to hear it. As soon as the rest of the guests loaded onto the shuttle and Linda and Fred left, I fled out the back door. I heard Brad call my name, but I needed some time to evaluate my feelings. At least he was acting like he cared about me.

"What happened with Nathaniel?" I asked, not ready to get into my stuff with Brad.

"You mean besides what he thought he saw going on with Brad?"

"Yeah. I don't understand him at all." I peeled the plastic wrap off the platter filled with slices of pound cake and placed a piece in each bowl.

She stopped mid-scoop and turned to face me. "Zoe, I'm so sorry. Please know I have no idea why he was behaving as if we were together. We agreed to be friends, and I assumed since you guys have been spending time together, you might not still be in the friend zone?" She finished the sentence like she was asking a question.

Before the events of the night, I'd had the answer, but as tears blurred my vision, I dropped my attention to the counter. The lump in my throat prevented me from saying anything without bursting into sobs. Apparently, I needed to do a little more than wallowing to get to the part where everything would be fine.

Wren dropped the ice cream scoop with a clank into the sink. "I'm such a terrible friend. I've been so caught up in the mural and Nathaniel that I haven't even asked you about Brad. I'm sorry."

Wiping my eyes, I swallowed away the lump. "We've all been busy, and to be honest, Brad and I have been keeping our relationship on the down-low to reduce the drama around here." I shrugged. "I guess we failed."

"So, what is going on with you two?"

"Good question, and I wish I had an answer. We agreed to keep things simple, no strings attached, but he keeps doing sweet things, like bringing me those flowers before the party."

She glanced at the bouquet. "He gave you those? Tonight? And then acted like you didn't exist with his parents?"

"Right? I know his parents are difficult, but his actions make me reconsider everything he's done. Is he just a nice guy who is confused about his feelings? Does he really not want more than friendship? When he kisses me, it certainly doesn't feel that way."

Wren piled heaps of ice cream on top of the pound cake. "You have such amazing chemistry, and I don't just mean the romantic kind." Smiling, she passed me a bowl. "I overheard something tonight that might cheer you up." Raising her brows teasingly, she turned without another word and went to the couch.

I hurried to join her. "What?"

"Cheryl told Linda that you and Brad were, and I quote, 'adorable together'." Wren nudged me.

"Really? Wow!" Ready to celebrate something, I put the yummy food in my mouth and was not disappointed. Sugary, buttery, creamy, and peachy flavors swirled over my tongue.

"Yes." Wren pointed her spoon at me. "She said something about how Brad is the rock to your whimsy."

"I guess that's a positive." But if Cheryl liked Brad's chemistry with me, what did that mean for Wren? The one time I claimed the spotlight, and I may have hurt a friend. A wave of nerves rippled through me. "When you went after Nathaniel, Linda insisted I step in. I hope that's okay."

"Absolutely. While I might have appeared all sunshine and roses, I wasn't in a good place."

"Oh, no. Was he furious?" I asked.

"Yes, mostly because I hadn't mentioned the TV show. Maybe I can tell him not to worry because Cheryl wants you and Brad."

"Absolutely not. We're a package deal." I clinked her bowl with mine. While I might've learned that I could lead a team to success, I loved working with Wren, and I didn't want to consider doing this job without her. "Besides, you'll probably need to be the rock to my whimsy because in a very odd turn of events, Brad is actually with Nathaniel on this one."

"I can't imagine them agreeing on anything."

"They probably have more in common than they'd admit, but the show specifically. Brad's dad hates the shows and the network, so Brad is totally against it too."

"What is the deal with his dad? I get that Brad's trying to prove himself. But he's a grown man. Surely, his dad will come around with something this big." Wren jabbed her spoon into the ice cream.

"I don't know, and it doesn't matter because Brad would never even talk to him about it."

"Well, like I told Nathaniel, nothing concrete has happened to suggest the show will happen."

"Surely the improbability eased his concerns," I offered.

"Nope, he accused me of thinking of my career before him and Haslemere. He actually said I was selfish." Her voice trailed off, like she might believe him. What a creep!

"Wren, you're the farthest thing from selfish." I stabbed the dessert. "You've gone out of your way to make him comfortable with the development plans, and as far as Haslemere, he's wrong. The town will benefit."

She shrugged. "You think so?"

"Of course. Don't listen to him. He writes romance novels, not business books. He's just afraid of change."

"Hopefully, once he calms down, we'll be able to have a civilized conversation."

"You mean once he apologizes."

"That would be nice, and I'm sure Brad will apologize to you and explain everything." She drew circles in her melting ice cream. "Can you believe we're almost finished with the house?"

"And it'll be months before we start on the clubhouse. I guess there isn't really a reason for us to be here." My gaze drifted to the bouquet. "I'd actually thought about staying and seeing where this thing with Brad might go when we weren't under so much pressure, but I don't know now."

"You really like him."

"Yeah. I've never had this kind of connection with a guy. He's totally different when it's just the two of us—so playful."

"Brad?" She eyed me skeptically.

"If I hadn't enjoyed every minute with the real him, I wouldn't have believed it. I keep hoping his dad will acknowledge what a brilliant manager Brad is."

She spared me a half-hearted smile. "I really hope it works out for you guys."

"Don't worry." After setting my spoon down, I wrapped my arm around her. "I'm sure Nathaniel will come around. He adores you."

"I don't know. Things between us seem uncertain. Not to mention the location challenges."

"You'll figure something out." I squeezed her shoulder.

"We'll see." Wren selected a streaming service on her laptop. "How about a movie about strong women and great friends? *Fried Green Tomatoes.* We'll laugh, we'll cry, and we'll remember why girls need each other."

"I'm totally up for that." Besides, if my dating life had taught me anything, it was that my happiness didn't equal being with Brad or any man. Sure, it could add variety, and kissing was fun, but I'd decided a long time ago that I wouldn't let a guy steal my sparkle.

Chapter Eleven

♥

Exhausted and with no reason to get up early, I'd turned off my alarms and snuggled in my bed, determined to sleep away as many hours as I could. Much to my satisfaction, which I was apparently setting a very low bar for these days, I'd slept well. When I finally woke, I contemplated the ceiling fan blades as they rotated.

In the living room, Wren sounded like she was hurrying around, and then I heard the door shut. Nathaniel had probably already messaged wanting to talk and hopefully apologize. I glanced at my phone on the bedside table but resisted the urge to check for a message from Brad. Linda and Fred were flying out early and had insisted that we all take a much-deserved day of rest on Sunday.

Before everything, I'd thought Brad and I might spend it together. We'd go to church, then have brunch and stroll the famous squares in Savannah before having an early dinner on the river with a sunset view.

If I believed I didn't need him, I'd get up, get dressed, and have that exact day on my own. But while it worked logically, I wasn't quite ready for logic, so I closed my eyes and settled on breathing deeply. I don't know how much time passed, but I had apparently accomplished the state known as deep relaxation when something interrupted my peace.

What was it? I scanned the room and listened. A faint knock registered. Brad? I rose as my very illogical pulse accelerated and my equally traitorous heart flipped.

Not today, body. I shook my arms and legs, releasing the nervous energy. How had I been so relaxed only moments before?

The knocking continued, so I shuffled to the cottage door and opened it.

"Morning." At least he hadn't tried to make it *good* and had the decency to look pretty terrible. The normally bright-eyed and charming man I'd almost let myself fall for gave me a half smile, his eyes dull with dark circles under them. "I know it's a little late, but I thought you might want to sleep in, and I didn't want to wake you." He lifted a basket. "I brought breakfast."

The scent of cinnamon and brown sugar drifted from the basket, tempting me, but I held my ground, glaring at him. I even pursed my lips, but unfortunately, my stomach was having none of it and announced with a loud grumble that it would like a taste of whatever was in the basket.

To his credit, his facial expression remained neutral, which in hindsight, should've been a clue of what he planned to do. "May I come in?"

Without answering, I took a seat at the small table with the flowers still in the middle, reminding me that the night before hadn't been a dream or a nightmare but worse—my real life.

"Thanks." Brad unloaded two travel cups of coffee. "I already put cream and sugar and a sprinkle of cinnamon in yours." Then he removed the top of a pastry box. Inside were squares of what my senses told me would be a decadent coffee cake.

Unwilling to let my pride force me to miss something delicious, I placed a piece on a napkin. "Thank you for breakfast," I said as evenly as possible. Maybe he'd leave, but did I want him to? Maybe, but first I wanted an explanation. I pinched off a corner of the cake and popped it into my mouth. The expected flavors, plus a lot of butter, melted over my tongue.

"It was the least I could do." He removed the lid from his cup of coffee, but he didn't serve himself any of the cake.

My skin prickled, alerting, but since I'd apparently been wrong about a lot lately, I ignored my intuition and sipped my coffee. "The cake is tasty." And so was the coffee. Of course he'd gotten it just right because he knew me and had taken the time to learn what I liked. Surely that was a good sign.

"I'm glad you like it."

"Aren't you going to have a piece?"

"Maybe later."

"Okay." I ate another bite, chewing it slowly, willing him to say something that would eliminate this awkwardness and make everything okay.

But instead, he sighed and scrutinized his coffee like he might find the answer there. "I'm sorry for everything. I tried to warn you before the party."

Was that what he'd meant? If he'd wanted me to understand his intentions, he probably shouldn't have kissed me silly. "Sorry, if I didn't understand your warning meant that I should've been prepared for you to turn into another person and make Wren your girlfriend less than an hour after you locked your lips with mine." I'd meant to soften my response, but I sounded bitter.

He shifted his attention to me but didn't look me in the eye. "You're right. I should've been clearer, and I should've insisted on better boundaries. When we were just friends, everything was less complicated, and I know it's my fault that things changed between us when they did. I thought if we moved slowly, it would be okay, and like you said, you didn't even know your future. But here's the problem. I *am* thinking about the future and the past. And I'm tired of being seen as an irresponsible teenager by my parents."

"I get that, but they seemed pleased with the project. And I still don't understand what that has to do with Wren."

"It doesn't, really, except that I told them we'd gone on a couple of dates, and they liked the idea, so I never told them we decided to just be friends." He rubbed his forehead.

"Why not?"

Brad pressed his palms on his shorts. "When I was in college, I met a girl at a party. Her name was Autumn, and she immediately captivated me. School already wasn't a priority for me, and it definitely wasn't for her. I'd always loved being the life of the party both metaphorically and literally. I guess you've seen a little of that side of me."

"And I like it."

"Yeah, well, it's not sustainable. Autumn and I were the worst thing for each other, but we were having a blast ruining our futures. At least we thought we were. We validated each other's poor choices. You don't need all the details, but as one skipped class led to a week of skipped classes, I failed out. Autumn's parents insisted she come home, and I didn't have any money or a job, so I had no other choice than to do the same. We tried the long-distance thing, but our relationship was pretty shallow, so it fizzled out."

"But that was years ago, and you've obviously changed. Maybe even gone too far in the other direction."

"Not possible, and my fling with Autumn was just the icing on the cake. I'd barely gotten accepted to college, and with the other trouble I'd gotten into in high school, my parents had warned me it would be my only chance to get a degree. But I didn't understand what that meant. I know they seem overbearing and judgmental, but I earned every bit of their doubt. Anyway, once I was working on one of my dad's crews and living at home with all of my friends away at school, I finally realized what I'd done. But I also realized that I liked the work. I enjoyed building things and eventually leading the team. I've been secretly finishing my business degree and will graduate at the end of the semester."

"That's fantastic. Congratulations."

"Thanks." He pressed his lips into a tight smile. "I wanted to show my parents that I had my life together—job, college, and wife. My perfect sister isn't married, so I could finally give my parents, especially my mom, the total package. I could be someone different in their eyes, and my dad would finally let me take over the company. It's been my dream for a long time. Everything I've been working for. I had it all planned out."

"But Wren isn't with you." And what was the deal with his sister?

"I understand that, and I tried to think of a way to tell them I'd dated both of you without it sounding flaky, but I couldn't. And the look on my mom's face when I told her Wren and I had gone out—I just wanted to hold on to that a little longer. I knew I'd have to tell her eventually, but also telling her that I'd given up the serious woman for the one covered in sparkles—I couldn't do it. I'm sorry, but it's nice to have them tell me that they're proud of me. Zoe, I think you're amazing, and your friendship has been more than I could have hoped for, and I don't want to mess that up."

What was he doing? Was he really trying to put us back in the friend zone?

He continued, "We've had some good times, but right now—"

"Stop." I stood. "It doesn't matter. I'm not changing, not today and not in the future. I did that once to save a relationship, and I won't do it again. Not that you're even asking." I paused for a moment to give him a chance to correct me.

His head shook slightly.

"Okay, well, I'm not sure how you're going to explain to your parents that you don't have the *perfect* wife lined up, but I won't mess things up for you. Believe it or not, I want you to succeed, and I think you deserve to run your family business. In fact, I think you'll be great at it, so I won't hold you back. And I'll help make this project a huge success. But I don't think we can go back to just being friends." I pivoted and strode to my bedroom.

Clutching the doorknob, I stopped and waited. Surely, he'd ask me to reconsider. And what would I say? Did I really want to be with someone who couldn't introduce me to his parents? But he needed to realize what he was giving up because being friends wasn't an option.

Then I heard his chair legs scrape over the tiled floor, and my heart leapt. This was it. He'd apologize, and we could kiss and make up. It'd be fine—

But his footsteps weren't approaching, so I slipped into the bedroom and firmly shut the door.

Over the next five days, I laughed and danced and fluffed pillows with the enthusiasm of someone who was blissfully living life, but it didn't lift my heavy heart. I should've given in and sought advice from Bonnie or at least shared another bowl of ice cream with Wren, but I didn't want to burden them. It'd been ridiculous to believe that I could attain both professional and personal success at the same time. What I should've done was plan my return to Chicago and taken a few days to visit my family in the burbs. But what I did was double down on my efforts to convince myself that I was fine without Brad, so I booked a week at the Kensley House in Haslemere.

At least I'd been given a reprieve from seeing him every day. He'd moved on to another project while Wren and I installed furniture and perfected the decor on the second story. In the meantime, I'd clung to the hope that time really healed all wounds because in a few months we'd be working on the clubhouse project. Perhaps worse, I was still dreaming about hosting a show on the Living Well Network.

It could happen. Exes partnered all the time, and we weren't even really that. It shouldn't be a problem to be completely over him by the time we started working together again. If I just kept pretending I was fine and he didn't matter, surely it'd eventually be reality.

What I hadn't anticipated was Wren suddenly booking a flight for Saturday afternoon. I don't know why it caught me off guard that she might pack up and leave. Only a couple of days before, she'd mentioned her mom needed her help, and I'd offered to handle the final details at Magnolia Bluff.

Still I'd thought her feelings for Nathaniel would outweigh her parents' control, or was I projecting my suppressed hopes for a change in Brad?

What?

Nope. I didn't have any hopes, suppressed, or otherwise.

"I won't be needing those." Wren shoved the box of painting supplies that Nathaniel had given her against the wall. Do you mind dealing with them?"

"Are you sure?" I moved out of her way as she rolled her suitcase to the front door. "Your paintings are beautiful, and I thought you were enjoying creating. The mural in the dining room was certainly a success. Everyone at the reveal party was talking about it."

"I can get new supplies in Chicago if I need them. I don't want those." She pointed at the box like it held her worst nightmares.

"I'm sorry you and Nathaniel hit a rocky patch, but surely you can work it out. It can't be that bad."

"I wish you were right, and if I could get past what happened, I would." She'd said nothing about her fallout with Nathaniel on Thursday and stayed locked in her room all day Friday. I only knew something had gone wrong because Bonnie had texted to check on her this morning.

"Do you want to talk about it?"

"It's not my story to tell." She sighed. Which was exactly what Bonnie had said when I'd asked her what had happened.

"Well, I'm here if you need me, and I'll take care of everything left on the project."

"You've really grown on this one, and I appreciate you taking on the extra responsibilities. You don't need me, especially when you have Brad. You guys are going to do great things together."

"We'll see." I refused to give her words much thought. I wanted to keep the focus on her. "Are you sure there isn't anything I can do?"

"You're doing enough, letting me leave with no concerns about the project. I need to get home and spend some time processing how I'm going to proceed. It's part of the last challenge from my grandmother." During our time at Magnolia Bluff, Wren had been completing a list of challenges her grandmother had left in her will.

"Then I'm sure it will help you. Your grandmother knew exactly what you needed."

"Until recently, I thought the same thing. Now I'm not so sure."

I wanted to ask for more details, but there was a knock at the door. Unlike the night of the party, this time I prayed it would be Nathaniel. Hopefully, he'd come to stop her and fix whatever had broken between them.

But when Wren opened the door, Brad stood outside. What was he doing here?

"Thanks so much for coming to get me," Wren said.

"Are you ready?" He entered, his gaze landing on me.

"Hi." I waved, but I couldn't say anything else as my insides knotted. Brad must have been her only choice for a ride with Nathaniel, and apparently Bonnie, out of the picture.

"Hi," he responded but shifted his attention from me. "Let me take your suitcase."

"All set." Wren hooked her bag over her shoulder, ignoring the awkward tension swirling around the room. "Call me if you need anything." She hugged me.

"Same." I squeezed her back.

Without another word and before I fully realized what was happening, Wren and Brad exited the cottage.

Then, in the silence, arrows of loneliness and regret pierced my heart. I rubbed my chest, trying to dull the ache. What had I done? Why couldn't I give Brad a chance? We could've been friends. He needed more time. Why couldn't I even meet him halfway?

But he'd hurt me, and he didn't fight for me.

Wren was right. Brad and I were great together, but now, he could barely speak to me. And because I'd insisted I was fine, I was stuck near him for at least two more weeks. Too close to heal and let things go. Logic said that I didn't have to see him, probably wouldn't, but my heart would know he was near, and it pushed hard against the walls of my chest, trying to escape.

But it couldn't, and there wasn't anything I could do to release the pain, so I let it hurt. For the first time since I'd closed the door on our future, I wrapped my arms around my body as the tears fell and I dropped to the ground. I wasn't fine. This wasn't fine. But it was still over.

And then I did the thing that I should've been doing all along—I prayed.

Chapter Twelve

♥

Almost a week later, I resigned myself to living the rest of my life a little less happy because my plan to fake it till I made it wasn't working at all. I hadn't expected it to, and I was almost okay. I could still find ways to sparkle. But maybe not as bright.

I focused my energies on my old go-to, baking. Also, I was now praying more than a monk. Actually, a monk, who'd taken a vow to bake and decorate houses and breathe like Virginia had taught me, perfectly described the way I spent my days during that week.

And I'd made it. Once I finished the walkthrough with Linda, I could move into the bed-and-breakfast. For a few blessed days, I'd alter my monk routine to a vow of silence and seclusion, and I might only talk to Jesus. Everything would be fine, better than fine, wonderful.

"Zoe, I can't say enough how absolutely thrilled I am with the results." Linda leaned against the counter in the kitchen. "You were so thoughtful to fill the pantry and fridge with some necessities and Southern delicacies. Thank you."

"You're welcome." I'd asked Bonnie to send over some recipes, and when she'd taken me to the store to stock up on ingredients, I'd questioned her about Nathaniel. But she declined to answer. Although she'd made it clear, he was suffering miserably and planning to win Wren back. Then she muttered something about marathon town meetings and being thankful for a break. Failing to see the relevance, I ignored her comment, which I'd learn later was a mistake, but that's a story for another day.

Instead, I told her to let him know if I could help, and she agreed, but he hadn't called, so I'd added Wren and Nathaniel to my prayer list. With my new recipes, I'd spent every night distracting myself in a flour and sugar haze before taking a few deep breaths and asking for God's peace and, if possible, a little wisdom. While faking happiness wasn't working, I'd started to find acceptance.

Linda removed the glass dome from the cake stand. "Please tell me you'll stay and have a slice of cake to celebrate with me."

The night before, feeling brave, I'd made Brad's Nana's hummingbird cake. It'd taken a lot of prayer, but as I arranged the roasted pecans around the top of the cake, a flutter of hope tickled my heart.

Don't get me wrong, I still regretted everything that had gone down with Brad, but I could still enjoy a piece of this dessert. "I'm glad you asked because I wanted to taste it."

Linda narrowed her eyes, studying me. "Something's wrong."

I shook my head, but she'd stated it with such certainty that I didn't have time to hide my frown. "Everything's fine."

"I'm not buying it." She scanned the house like she was searching for something before her gaze settled back on me. "I understood Wren had to return to Chicago for her family, but I'm surprised Brad isn't here."

"I think he's busy with another project."

"You think? Hmm." She pointed to a chair at the kitchen table. "Have a seat while I get the cake and give you a chance to decide if you want to tell me what happened. And while you ponder your decision, I'll tell you what I think." Linda retrieved plates from the cabinet and placed them on the counter. "Because when I was here last, it seemed you and our contractor had at the very least developed a strong friendship. But in my experience, people who are just friends don't have a reason to stop communicating, so I'd expect you to know whether he's busy." She sliced two pieces of cake and arranged them on the plates. "Which means something else was going on." She put a piece of cake and a fork in front of me. "So do you want to tell me?"

"It seems unprofessional to burden you with the drama of my failed love life." *Oops.* I scooped a large bite of cake onto my fork and shoved it in my mouth before I blurted anything else.

"As I expected, but I don't understand. You guys had such great chemistry that even Cheryl commented on it."

"Wren told me, and I think we'll be fine as friends. We need this time apart to downshift." There that sounded mature.

"But why would you do that?"

"It's what's best."

"For who?"

"For the development and the show and definitely Brad's business."

"Aha. Now we're getting to the crux of the matter."

"I shouldn't have said that. Please forget it." I pressed my palm over my face. It's a good thing I wasn't responsible for keeping government secrets. But since I'd already shared too much, I needed to do damage control, so I continued, "I promise none of this will impact our future projects. In fact, if you want, I can step away, but please don't cancel the contracts with Chastain Construction because of me. If you do, Mr. Chastain will never turn over the business to Brad."

"Calm down, Zoe." Linda gently pulled my hand away from my head. "Don't worry. I'm not going to pull the contracts from the Chastains, and I won't let you quit. All of you have more than proven yourselves."

"Thank you." I pushed my chair back from the table. "I'll just head out. My bags are packed, and I had a rental car delivered yesterday, so I'll be out of your hair in no time."

"Hold on. Is your flight soon?"

"Um, no, actually, I'm staying at the bed-and-breakfast in Haslemere for a week."

"So there's no rush?"

I gripped my knees. "Not really, but—"

"Fantastic." Beaming, Linda flung her palms out in front of her. "Then we have at a minimum seven days to fix all of this."

"I don't think there's anything to fix."

"Nonsense. Anyone with eyes could see how much Brad adores you, and you him."

"Really?"

"Yes, now tell me what went wrong while I enjoy my treat." She dug into her cake.

"Okay. Originally, Brad and I tried to stay in the friend zone, but well, we were drawn to each other in a way I'd never expected or experienced. Brad was different with me when we were on our own. He listened to me and made me feel special. But on the night of the reveal party, he basically ignored me and acted like he was with Wren. His parents, especially his dad, don't show him a lot of respect."

"Unbelievable. Brad's been amazing to work with, so diligent and proactive. He's gone above and beyond to make this project a success. I wish I'd known. I could've said something, but I barely spoke to them. Anyway, what does this have to do with Wren and you?" She filled her fork with another bite.

"He'd told them that he and Wren were dating, and they'd gone out a couple of times, but they decided they were best as friends and work colleagues. Anyway, Brad wants his dad to turn the business over to him, but his dad has been hesitant at best. Brad didn't want them to think he'd dated both of us."

"I see."

"I could've overlooked one unfortunate night, but he didn't see a future for us beyond being friends, because he doesn't think his parents approve of me. At least, not this version of me." I indicated my sequined headband. "I know I can seem a little whimsical, but I'm a hard worker, and when Wren was consumed with the mural, I led this project."

"And you did it well." She tapped her fork against her plate. "Did Brad say he wanted you to change?"

"He didn't say he didn't." Not that I'd given him much of a chance to, but he had done nothing to stop me or make me think he wanted anything different.

"Interesting, and I'm guessing you haven't reached out to him to seek understanding or some kind of compromise."

"I'm not changing. When I was in college, I did everything for this guy I had a crush on, including all the work on our class project. It was an *A* project, but our professor had us evaluate each other. Well, apparently, my crush didn't think I was so impressive. He described me as immature and my ideas as vacuous. As evidence, he pointed out my style of dressing like a fairy—even though, for the presentation, I'd dressed conservatively like he'd requested. He used that against me too, reporting that he'd had to keep me in line like a child and practically chose my outfit. The whole time he'd acted like he was into me. I've kept guys at a safe distance since then." I folded my arms around my waist, emotions clambering to work their way to the surface, and I'd been unprofessional enough today without dissolving into tears.

"That's terrible, but Zoe—" Linda shifted, giving me her full attention— "Brad is not that guy. Brad has never taken credit for your work."

"But he didn't tell his parents what I did on the project. On the night of the party, they thought Wren was the lead designer, and I was her assistant."

"Okay. I'm not saying that Brad doesn't need to apologize and set his parents straight, but surely there's some middle ground where you can meet."

"I wish, but I don't think his dad can see past what is right in front of his face, and I don't want to mess up Brad's career. It's really important to him."

"Everything I hear you saying sounds like you care deeply for Brad. I understand you don't want to sacrifice yourself for the relationship, and you shouldn't, but what if there was another way?"

"I mean, I've tried for two weeks to get over him, so I guess I'd do a lot to find a way, but I don't want to lose myself in the process."

"I seriously doubt Brad wants that either. While your style is important, it's not all there is to you, and it's unlikely Brad only sees you as an encouraging work friend. You said he was different around you. It's not a leap to believe his feelings for you run deep and are based on a lot more than your sparkly persona and how you could help him."

"But what if it isn't enough?" I worried my lip. I'd taken the comfortable position as cheerleader for my friend, but what if he didn't see me as more?

"Love doesn't make you change, but it can make you better, and from what I saw of you together, you complete each other. At the very least, you complete each other's sentences." She smirked.

I chuckled, and for the first time since I'd closed my bedroom door, I felt like I could help Brad achieve his goal *and* have a future with him. Linda was the last person I'd expected to be the answer to my prayers, but apparently, God did work in incomprehensible ways, and I was ready to take a step of faith.

"You think there really might be another way?" I said.

Linda tapped her fingers together, mastermind style. "Absolutely."

"And you think we can make it happen in a week, and we won't hurt Brad's chances with his dad?"

"Absolutely. If Brad's dad isn't telling the world how great you are and how pleased he is to have you dating his son by the end of the week, I'll help Brad set up his own company and hire him."

"Wow. Okay, but I hope we don't disappoint you."

"I'm not even a little concerned. One of the reasons I've been successful is because I know a good thing when I see it, and all of this is brimming with possibilities."

Possibilities. The very word eased my concern, not to mention Linda's enthusiasm, so we plotted a way to make all our dreams come true.

Knowing I couldn't show up empty-handed and being pretty certain that the best way to soften up a man was through his stomach, I baked blueberry muffins with a streusel topping. I wasn't sure if streusel was popular in the South, but I loved the topping on muffins, so I hoped it would delight—or at least intrigue—Mr. Chastain and not offend his traditional sensibilities.

Then again, perhaps I was projecting my hopes for his change of opinion about me onto muffins.

At this point, it didn't matter because I couldn't turn back. Well, technically, no one had seen me yet, so I could make a run for it. But facing Linda if I failed to follow through with her plan seemed slightly scarier than my impending encounter with Mr. Chastain.

Once I'd given Linda the go-ahead, she'd morphed into a military strategist and provided a course of action that she assured me would be successful. After all, she said, all's fair in love and war.

The plan had two prongs. First, Linda would contact Mr. Chastain, gushing with praise for Brad. And to prove how confident she was, she picked up her phone and called Brad's dad on the spot. She described in detail how wonderful Brad was to work with and how much she looked forward to having him on her team for the clubhouse project. As if that wasn't enough, she told him she'd be recommending Brad to all the potential Magnolia Bluff homeowners, regardless of whether he was with Chastain Construction.

At the hint, Mr. Chastain assured Linda that Brad was an integral part of the operation, and he appreciated her business. With a satisfied smirk, Linda had ended the call and told me that he was ready for the next step in the battle plan.

And that's how I ended up standing outside the offices of Chastain Construction with a platter of muffins, running through my breathing exercises and praying for strength as I fulfilled part two in Linda's scheme.

On my final exhale, I rolled back my shoulders and strode through the door. After the receptionist greeted me, and I gave her a muffin, I told her who I was and asked to speak with Mr. Chastain. My pulse raced as she called him. What if he wouldn't meet with me? I hadn't even considered the possibility because Linda had been so sure her strategy was flawless.

"Tell him Linda from the Retreat at Magnolia Bluff wanted me to stop by," I interrupted the receptionist as she spoke to Mr. Chastain.

It might have been underhanded, but it worked, and within seconds, Mr. Chastain was ushering me into his office. "Zoe, it was so kind of you to drop by. Will Linda be joining us?"

"Not today."

"That's too bad. We had a nice chat the other day."

"That's what she said." I held out the tray, willing my hands not to shake. "I made a batch of blueberry muffins for you."

"That was thoughtful. Thank you." He placed the muffins on his desk. "Please have a seat. I'm not sure what I've done to deserve baked goods, but I make it a practice to never turn down a homemade treat."

Muffins for the win!

And before I could overthink it, I clasped my trembling fingers together. "I hope you enjoy them, and you earned them by raising a remarkable man."

His brows shot up, but I didn't give him a chance to respond.

"Not only is Brad amazing at his job and a strong project leader, but he is a man of integrity. He puts everyone's needs and wants ahead of his own, and you need to take off your blinders and see him for the man he is and not the boy he once was." Running out of breath, I paused.

"Well, this is unexpected."

I shook my head, my dangly earrings jingling. "I'm not finished. You may think I'm flamboyant and silly, and that's fine. But Brad and I developed a special friendship while we were working on the Magnolia Bluff project, and because of our commitment to success, we agreed not to get serious. Of course, it didn't work. Turns out hearts are harder to manage than a host of subcontractors. Anyway, it wasn't Wren who Brad was spending his very limited spare time with. It was me, and we were good together, great actually. But because Brad didn't think you'd approve of me, he was willing to sacrifice our relationship and his happiness to please you."

"I see."

"I hope so, and I hope you'll consider bringing Brad on as an equal partner. He is the future of Chastain Construction, but you have to give him a chance. It'd also help if you'd show a little faith in him and show him some gratitude for the job he's doing."

I moved to the edge of my seat and pressed my damp palms against my knees. "Thank you for listening to me. I hope you enjoy the muffins." I rose, swallowing down the nervous tickle that might manifest as giggles if I didn't get control of myself.

"Before you go, you should probably know that Brad has been singing your praises as well." He stood. "I didn't understand why until now, and I appreciate your honesty. It seems I have a lot to think about."

It wasn't the response I'd been expecting. Actually, I hadn't let myself think about what he might say, so I simply nodded and turned for the door. When I was safely inside my rental car, relief ricocheted through me, and I released everything in an explosion of giggles.

If nothing else, I hoped Brad's dad would wake up and see how important Brad was to his business. As far as my future with Brad, Linda had assured me it would work itself out, and really, I wanted to give Mr. Chastain and Brad a chance to deal with their issues before we reconnected. Brad needed to have some candid conversations with his parents before he'd be ready to be with me or I'd be willing to give him my heart again. Not that I believed he didn't already have it. I just hoped he'd be more careful with it in the future, and if not, I prayed God would heal it.

It was strange, the peace that filled me as I went through the next couple of days. Although it helped that I was exhausted in all the ways, the calm had more to do with me fully surrendering my future with Brad to God. Some people might claim that I didn't have a choice, but they hadn't encountered the force that was Linda. If I'd wanted to grab control of the situation and force my timing, Linda certainly would have devised another plan of attack.

Of course, she didn't let me avoid her for long. The day after my meeting with Mr. Chastain, she texted me while I was eating breakfast.

> Linda: Good morning! Fred won't be here until the end of the week, and I'm so lonely out here with all this peace and quiet. Will you join me for dinner? We can catch up, and you can give me an update on Mission: Win Brad Back.

I wasn't sure when she'd come up with the name, but it brushed away some of my anxiety. It felt good to have someone to share my secrets with.

Although I might've been better served to find someone less ambitious, Bonnie was unavailable because whatever Nathaniel was plotting to win Wren back was taking up all her time. I should've commiserated with him, but then again, he had the entire town wrapped up in his business. If Linda was a lot, the citizens of Haslemere had to be overwhelming.

> Me: Sure! I'd offer to bring dessert, but I no longer have a kitchen.

> Linda: You don't need to bring anything, but let's dress up a little!

> Me: Even better. I never pass up an opportunity to get fancy!

> Linda: Fantastic. 6:30 sharp.

> Me: Sure. Thanks!

Was she always so bossy with her invitations? Maybe, but I didn't care.

I popped the last bite of the biscuit with peach preserves in my mouth, enjoying the way the salty butter danced with the sweetness of the peaches. This was a time to savor my blessings, and after a stroll through the gardens surrounding the Kensley House, I'd put together an ensemble to impress Linda. Then I might lounge on the porch swing and watch the butterflies and hummingbirds.

Before I'd moved into the inn, I hadn't realized how much stress I'd been under. But I'd discovered so much about myself and found courage I didn't know I possessed. Only a few weeks earlier, I'd have never considered confronting a man like Mr. Chastain or moving away from my family, but now, anything seemed possible.

With that delightful, carefree spirit, I twirled once in my shimmery aqua sundress as I waited for Linda to answer the door the next night.

The rays of the setting sun made the iridescent material change colors. It reminded me of a mermaid's tail. I could take a trip to the beach. It was so close. I should ask the innkeepers where I could find the best shells.

As the front door opened, I gave the short skirt a swoosh, watching a rainbow appear on the white planter boxes. "Isn't that lovely? I don't understand why sequins and glitter aren't a part of everyone's everyday wardrobe." I glanced up, but my eyes didn't meet Linda's.

Instead, my breath caught, and I think my heart stuttered before it started drumming like it was trying to catch up to the beat it'd missed.

Brad smiled, his eyes taking me in like I was a slice of a seven-layer chocolate cake. "Hi," he said, holding my gaze.

I'm sure the world kept on turning, but for a moment, time stood still. Then my pulse settled into a steady, albeit upbeat, rhythm as I inhaled a shaky breath. With oxygen feeding my brain again, I blinked twice to be sure he wasn't a figment of my imagination. But he was still there, a curious brow ticking up slightly above his twinkling left eye.

Then I pinched the inside of my wrist because I had to be dreaming. He was basically the star of my dreams every night, so it made sense. But the pinch hurt, and now he tilted his head, studying me, so I did the only thing I could think to do. I brushed my fingers over the back of his hand, sending sweet tingles up my arms. Both of them, even though I only touched him with two fingers. Yes! He was definitely real!

Before I could pull my hand to my side, Brad caught it. "Zoe, are you okay?"

"Mm-hm." I nodded, warmth filling me.

"Do you want to come inside? I've got some things I need to tell you." He tugged gently.

"You do?"

"Yes, and Linda helped me arrange all of this. She said if you hesitated, to remind you of the mission."

When a tiny giggle escaped from me, it took with it the last of my nervous tension. This was Brad, and he was here to tell me things, and I was all for it. "I guess I better come with you then."

Keeping our fingers intertwined, Brad led me to the dining room. "Before I say anything else, you look beautiful tonight. You always do." He pulled out two chairs, turning them to face each other.

"Thank you." I sat in one, while he took the other. "It's good to see you. I'm sorry I ended things before they could really get started. You said we shouldn't get serious, and that's not normally an issue for me, but—" I pressed my lips into a slight smile, not knowing what to say next.

What if he still just wanted to be friends? What if Linda was wrong? What if his dad fired him? What if I messed up everything?

Grimacing, I arched a brow at him, passing him the proverbial baton. With four siblings, you have things like talking batons. It's the only way everyone gets a chance to participate in the conversation. But what if Brad didn't understand? I peered at him wide-eyed, waiting.

"Please don't look so scared. Did you want to say something else?" he asked.

I shook my head.

"Okay, well, I'm sorry too. I shouldn't have put my career before you, and I should've been truthful with my parents. As soon as I left you the morning after the party, I regretted my choice. I should've come back. But what can I say? I wanted so desperately to be successful in my parents' eyes."

"You mentioned that before, but I guess I don't fully understand."

"Probably because it required me seeing my life and the relationship with my parents come full circle to comprehend what was motivating me to the extent that I'd give you up. It was my mom's eyes when I failed out of college with such reckless abandon. I'd seen her disappointed before. Frustrated, even angry. But you never forget the expression on the face of the one person who was always there for you, always believed in you, when she finally gives up on you."

When his attention dropped to our joined hands, my heart squeezed. He'd hurt me, but I hadn't appreciated the depth of his pain. In our ridiculous effort not to get serious, we'd avoided these types of conversations.

After a moment, he glanced up. "I realize now that'd been my turning point, and I've basically lived every day determined to erase that image and replace it with one of hope. The way she always looked when she talked about my sister. On the night of the party, I saw it when she saw the results and when I mentioned meeting Wren. I couldn't let it slip away. For once, they were bragging about me at church, and I wasn't the embarrassment they hid. Finally, my dad was saying things about me taking on more responsibilities and learning the business.

"For a moment, the redemption in my mom's face was almost enough, but I kept seeing your expectant eyes darkening with the realization that I was giving up on us. I knew I had to do something, but I didn't know what. I didn't want to hurt you again, but what I kept coming back to was that my future would not be very bright without your sparkle." He touched my face near my eye where I'd applied a bit of shimmery powder.

"Anyway, before I get distracted—" Brad clasped his knee, grinning— "you weren't the only one who let things get serious, and I don't want to just be friends, and I don't want you to change anything about you." He paused, taking a quick breath that he audibly blew out. "I think I love everything about you. I mean, I do, but that's kind of a lot, not you, I mean my feelings." He cringed and shifted his focus to the floor.

It was my turn to talk, and I was ready, so I squeezed his hand tighter, like it was that talking baton. "Your feelings are a lot, but I feel the same way."

"That's great news." He shifted his focus back to me.

"But what about your dad and the business?"

"You made quite an impression. He likes your spunk and thinks you're good for me. Also, I explained that you basically ran the show because Wren was painting the mural."

"Thanks for that, but I had a lot of help from the general contractor, and he deserves to be rewarded for his hard work."

"On that note, it turns out I hadn't been as clear as I'd thought I'd been about wanting to run the company. Dad thought I wanted him around to help, and I think I probably have a lot to learn before he turns over the reins completely, but now we're working on it."

"And your mom?"

"She wants to get to know you better, but I told her how much you love baking and antiques. Mostly, she said she just wants to see me happy and hopefully, settled." He cocked a brow. "But that's more than a lot for today, so why don't we just start with a celebratory dinner."

"Sounds good to me." Leaning forward, I clutched his shoulder. "Aren't kisses usually a part of making up?" I whispered against his cheek.

Thankfully, he responded by turning his head and catching my mouth with his as he pulled me into his lap. With our lips expressing the final surrender of our hearts, we melded together, embracing each other and what seemed like our future.

But in too short a time, Brad drew his lips from mine and kissed my cheek. "They're here."

"Who?" I opened my eyes, trying to focus on him.

"My parents. For supper. Linda helped me arrange the whole thing. Something about the third wave of her battle plan."

I straightened, grasping his shoulders. "Are you serious?"

"Yes." He shrugged. "And I almost forgot, we're also celebrating me graduating from college. I finished my last class."

"I-I don't know what to say."

"Most people stick with congratulations."

"Not about that, but congratulations."

"Oh, you mean my parents. That is a conundrum." He knitted his brow, but the corner of his lip twitched up. Was he about to laugh?

"Stop it. What if they come in and see us?" I swatted his shoulder and tried to shift off his lap.

"You're not running out of here." Brad held me tightly and pressed a kiss to my forehead. "Zoe, we aren't doing anything wrong, and from here on, we face hard things together."

"You think this will be hard?" My adrenaline was pumping now, but before I fled, all of his words registered. *We face hard things together*. I adored the sound of the *we* and the *together*, so I stayed.

I mean, I didn't stay in his lap. Before we called in his parents and Linda, but on threat of withholding kisses later, I convinced him to let me stand. Not that I would have followed through on the threat. Baking and antiques were great, but kissing Brad was the best.

Epilogue

♥

Sometimes the big blessings in life can lead to some terrifying things, and just when you think you've conquered your fear, you discover it's still lurking inside you. At least that's what my zipping pulse was communicating to me as Brad ordered champagne from the flight attendant assigned to our first-class cabin. Yes, first class, because when the Living Well Network books your flights, that is where you sit. This was not a blessing that led to scary things. Actually, it probably would, because if we had to move back to economy when this show thing blew up, I'd know what I was missing.

Closing my eyes, I inhaled deeply and counted silently before exhaling and then continuing the exercise. Through a lot of digging and the help of Laura—that's what Brad's mom told me to call her during our celebratory dinner with Linda that seemed like a lifetime ago, not less than a year—I'd found Virginia's contact information and sent her a thank you note. Being seated by that preschool teacher was not a coincidence, but a gift from God. That being said, I was currently questioning God's wisdom on the gifts he'd chosen to give me.

As I exhaled, Brad drew me under his arm. "Everything is going to be fine, Zoe."

His words, his embrace, they brought me a bit of comfort, but the idea of failing him, his business, my design firm, his parents, my parents,

Wren, our future children—I gasped for air, pressing my palm against my racing heart. Was I seriously going to have a panic attack?

"Zoe, breathe." Brad turned me to face him and gathered my hands in his. "Remember, we do hard things together."

I nodded as the wave of anxiety ebbed.

Over the months since Brad uttered those words the first time, we'd repeated them for big and little moments, some not hard at all, like deciding to help Nathaniel surprise Wren and my move to Savannah. Others were more challenging, like the decision to take the job promotion that made me the head of the new Savannah branch of the design firm. Not to mention the day we'd told his dad, Jim, about the screen test for the Living Well show. To our surprise, after he asked a lot of questions, he agreed to the idea with cautious optimism. For a while, I worried he'd change his mind, or Brad would, but the further we went, the more excited they were for the show.

"I love you." I settled my cheek against Brad's chest, letting the steady rhythm of his heartbeat soothe me. "Thank you for being my rock."

Actually, Brad's parents had been very supportive and encouraging. I still hadn't met his perfect sister Carleigh in person, but Brad rarely compared himself to her anymore. It helped that his parents complained about her absence and lack of communication, and Brad saw she wasn't so perfect. Trying on vintage engagement rings while shopping with Laura certainly didn't hurt our relationship. She pretended we should take our time, but I'd overheard her on the phone telling Carleigh that she hoped she'd at least make it home for her brother's wedding.

Brad tucked a ringlet over my ear and kissed my forehead. "I love you. If this show is going to stress you out, we can forget the whole thing."

"You know I don't want that. It's just sometimes when I think about all the people counting on me, I get overwhelmed."

"On us."

"What?"

"Us. It's not just you. I hope you're not including me on that list, because I'm right here, in it with you."

"I know, but I can't help it. You're always at the top of my list of people to worry about."

"I feel like that's a good thing, but at the same time, I want you to depend on me."

"I do. Without you, I'd have quit a long time ago. Honestly, I may have turned around and gotten back on the plane when I landed in Savannah without Wren."

"I'm really glad you stayed. It was definitely a turning point in my life. I just didn't know it at the time."

"Me too."

Our lives had changed a lot since Wren told me that Cheryl wanted Brad and me to be the stars of her next show, but a lot had stayed the same. We were still working on the clubhouse for the development and making plans for two more houses, but now we drove from Savannah to Magnolia Bluff together. And since we'd gone to California and signed the contracts for the show, Cheryl told us things would start moving faster.

We'd spent two days with network people. We'd met with a photographer for promotional pictures and a producer to discuss our project timelines. It'd all felt glamorous but also surreal, and I'd tried to soak up everything, but I'd never remember all of it. I was so glad to have Brad's hand around mine, reminding me that we were doing this together.

As much as I was enjoying living my dream, these quiet moments with Brad were becoming the favorite parts of my days. We'd spent a lot of time talking about our pasts, our worries, our dreams, our fears, and our families. All the things we'd left unsaid when we were pretending not to fall in love. And while I'd never consent to living even a second longer in the friend zone with Brad, I'm glad we had that time too. He was my best friend.

"Hey." Brad squeezed my shoulder. "Our drinks are coming."

"Are you going to make a cheesy toast? Because you know I'm here for it. The mushier the better." I shifted as Brad accepted the flutes from the flight attendant. Since we'd been dating seriously, which was pretty much from the moment Brad sat me down in Linda's dining room, he regularly declared his feelings for me and often with an audience. Even that night, he'd toasted me and our relationship with words that made everyone tear up, even the stoic Jim.

"I do have some words prepared. I'd planned to say them later, but this suddenly feels like the right moment." As he passed me my glass, his fingers trembled slightly. Was he nervous? Brad was almost always the picture of confidence. He confessed that he'd been nervous before he'd opened the door and seen me in my shimmery aqua sundress, but apparently, the way the light reflects off sparkly things eases his worries. Personally, I still think he believes I might be a fairy.

Why was he nervous now?

I shot my attention to him, my pulse picking up.

Brad held up a very sparkly vintage diamond engagement ring. "Zoe, we have a lot to celebrate, but most of all, before things get crazy, I want you to know that I celebrate the way you love me so well, and I celebrate the privilege I have to love you with everything I have. I celebrate our friendship, our work partnership, and our future family. I know this isn't the most romantic place for a proposal, but I couldn't wait. Will you marry me?"

I blinked, and then on cue, I started giggling.

Brad rolled his eyes. "Zoe, please, you're killing me."

"Oh, sorry, yes, of course I'll marry you." I held out my left hand.

Chuckling, Brad slipped the ring on my finger. "I'm glad this is the reaction I expected from you." He pressed his lips to mine, stopping the laughter and reminding me that we were so much more than friends.

When he pulled away, he tapped his glass to mine. "I love you, but I'm all tapped out of mushy things to say."

"I don't need you to say anything else, and if we weren't on this plane, I'd make sure you couldn't. But as future TV stars, we should probably keep things G-rated." I sipped my champagne. "Speaking of our busy schedule, I don't want to wait."

"Fine with me, but I don't want you stressed out either."

"Let's elope."

"Not a chance. My mom would never forgive us."

"True. So we'll keep it really small, and I'll let her plan it."

"Perfect. She'll love that, but you should have what you want."

"Don't you know that you're all I want?" I placed my hand on his cheek.

"I do, but it's nice to hear. You're all I want, too."

"I can do you one better." I gave him a coy smile. "I love you more than sequins and glitter." And I did. I'd probably even give them up for him, because loving someone meant knowing you'd sacrifice everything for him, but he wouldn't ask you to because he loved you as much as you loved him.

The End

Stealing Magnolias
Book 1 - Magnolia Bluff

When Wren Frazier heads south to honor her grandmother's final wish, she finds five unexpected challenges, one grumpy (but handsome) neighbor, and maybe—herself.

Although an artist, Wren packed away her brushes and paints and sought a practical career as an interior designer in Chicago. She's always put herself last, happy to please everyone around her. But with a team of dedicated co-workers and a small town of quirky characters supporting her, she's forced to give herself a little attention. As her artistic heart starts to awaken, Wren finds herself rediscovering the joy of creation and living authentically.

But while she's exploring the enchanting Georgia Low Country, creating beautiful paintings, and taking a chance on love, she uncovers a secret that shakes the foundation of her newfound happiness. With the revelation threatening to ruin the delicate balance Wren has only begun to realize, will she give up her fairytale and return to her reality?

About the Author

Award-winning author Leslie Kirby DeVooght writes women's fiction with faith, love, laughter, and a lot of Southern charm. Her stories are inspired by romcoms, coastal Georgia, and fried okra! When Leslie isn't writing, she volunteers with several organizations, cheers on her three children, and enjoys date nights with her husband, who loves that she researches kissing.

In addition to writing her own stories, Leslie co-owns *Spark Flash Fiction*, an online magazine that publishes romance collections of short, short stories. Check out Leslie's flash fiction stories on her website and join her newsletter for updates, giveaways, and early release opportunities (https://lesliedevooght.com/contact/). Keep in touch on Instagram (https://www.instagram.com/lesliedevooght/) and Facebook (https://www.facebook.com/LeslieDeVooght).

Leslie's debut novel, *Stealing Magnolias*, released in May 2025. Harlequin's Love Inspired imprint will publish Leslie's second book, *Taking a Second Shot*, on December 30, 2025.

Order *Stealing Magnolias* here: https://a.co/d/4KRlGHv

Order *Taking a Second Shot* here: https://a.co/d/1Kw8Mvd

Also by Leslie!

To make a little boy happy, they must team up.

Struggling professional soccer player Rainey Allen came to her grandparents' small town in Georgia to train—certainly not to coach kids. But when a grief-stricken boy gets excited about playing with her, she can't refuse. Even if his uncle is Scott Wilcox, the star player in Rainey's worst preteen memory. Once on track to be a pro athlete himself, Scott is grappling with his new life as the high school baseball coach and guardian of his orphaned nephew. But as playing soccer puts the light back in Henry's eyes, old wounds begin to heal. When Rainey gets her big break, will she give up on her dreams...or leave behind the family who stole her heart?

Acknowledgements

Thank you to everyone who has celebrated and encouraged the Magnolia Bluff series! All of your reviews have kept me going. I pray that my words bless you.

To my mother-in-law Diane, who purchased every faux magnolia in Jacksonville and shares my stories with everyone, I can't express how grateful I am to have you on my team. Thank you to my parents for their support and encouragement. Maybe Ainsley will read my book.

Thank you to my writing friends, especially my editor, Laurie Sibley, and assistant, Heather Tabers. Once again, the beautiful cover design is thanks to the talented Emily Singleton. (Stay off those mountain bikes!)

Thank you to my kids who have the privilege of popping into bookstores with me and letting me record and take pictures. To Kirby, thank you for making silly videos with me and trying to help me with tik-tok. Thank you to Charlie for being the best cashier. Thank you to Libby for proofreading my story and toning done my vocabulary.

Carlton, I wouldn't be able to write without your support both practical and emotional. One day will figure out publisher rocket and maybe will actually break even. Thank you for reminding me that my job is a mission and the results just look different.

There is nothing I can do without God. This powerful lesson I re-learn every time I start a story. I am so grateful that He has given me this opportunity to do what I love. Thank you Jesus for for always filling me with hope and love!

9 781967 524020